Welcome to Washington, Fina Mendoza

Kitty Felde

Black Rose Writing | Texas

ISBN: 978-1-68433-223-6
PUBLISHED BY BLACK ROSE WRITING
www.blackrosewriting.com

Printed in the United States of America
Suggested Retail Price (SRP) $17.95

Welcome to Washington, Fina Mendoza
is printed in Palatino Linotype

Cover art courtesy of Imelda Hinojosa

Welcome to Washington, Fina Mendoza

Chapter One

"There's no such thing as a Demon Cat of Capitol Hill."

That's what Papa would say, and he should know. Papa's a big deal congressman, the smartest person in Washington, D.C. But Papa wasn't down here in the Crypt. Nobody was here but me and a circle of statues, all of them Founding Fathers I'd never heard of from states I'd never visited. Like Caesar Rodney from Delaware, a guy who signed the Declaration of Independence who scowled at me from across the room. I felt those marble eyes staring as if they were saying, "You wouldn't even be in the Crypt after visiting hours, Fina Mendoza, if you hadn't lost your school sweatshirt. Again."

That hoodie had to be somewhere. My mom used to say "retrace your steps" whenever I lost something, which was pretty often. "Where were you the last time you had it?" she'd ask.

I tried to remember. I knew I was wearing it after school, when I shuffled through the leaves in the park across the street. I remembered finding a perfectly shaped golden leaf and sticking it in the sweatshirt pocket. Then what? Did I leave it somewhere in the U.S.

Capitol? The fleece wasn't back at the X-ray machine at the south door. I already looked. Maybe it was up on the third floor in Papa's Rules Committee room. But I didn't think so. Where else to look? The Capitol Crypt.

The Crypt wasn't a friendly room. It might be convenient, smack in the middle of the Capitol building with doorways leading everywhere. But it wasn't a place that invited you to stick around and make yourself comfortable. Stone floors and stone columns made it a cold place. During the day, it was crowded with school groups, kids wearing matching neon green tee shirts. Those kids ignored the tour guides and made fun of the exhibits. They never looked at the ancient wooden clock from the old House chamber. They walked right past the replica of the Magna Carta inside its giant plastic box.

The one thing they did like was the miniature model of the National Mall. It was one of the few things in the Capitol that you could touch without getting yelled at. Tiny white plastic versions of the Lincoln Memorial and the U.S. Capitol sat at opposite ends on top of a long table. In between, there were miniature memorials and monuments and museums on the Mall. It was my favorite thing in the Capitol, too.

That's why I came to the Crypt this afternoon. I wanted to memorize every building on the National Mall so that I would know as much about Washington as Papa. The table was just my height. I could look from one end of the Mall to the other without standing on tiptoe.

Of course, there was another reason I was in the

Capitol Crypt: I had no place else to go. My sister Gabby had band practice, marching around her high school football field with a clarinet. My grandmother was coming east to take care of us, but not for another two weeks. Until then, I had to come straight to the Capitol after school and wait until Papa finished working. Papa said I could go over to a friend's house to do homework. But after a month at my new school, I still didn't have a single new friend.

So I came to the Crypt, to study the model of the National Mall. There was something weird about it. There were *two* Washington Monuments right in the middle. I don't know why. I wanted to ask Papa about it. But first, I had to find my sweatshirt.

I started my search by circling the room, ignoring those Founding Fathers watching my every move. The Crypt was dark and echoey in the late afternoon. Strange shadows painted the arched ceiling. The ancient air conditioner wheezed as if it was about to die at any moment. The Crypt never felt scary in the middle of the day when tour guides in red jackets used their outside voices, warning kids not to lean on the display cases. Now all those bored eighth graders were back on buses, going home to Pennsylvania or Delaware or New Jersey. All the tour guides had traded in their official red jackets for overcoats and scarves and were heading to the Metro. It was just me here in the Crypt. Me...and something else.

I felt a tingling behind my ears, a sense that I wasn't alone. I looked behind me. Nothing was there. "Hello?"

I said, trying not to squeak. There was no answer.

The saucer-shaped ceiling lights were turned down low. Anything could be hiding behind the fat columns. Anything. My navy fleece wasn't here, but something else was.

I tried again. "Hello?"

Don't be a baby, Fina, I told myself. You're ten years old now. Or "double digits" as my sister Gabby called it. You're too old to be afraid of the dark. Don't be a scaredy-cat. I tried to stand a little bit taller, but that's hard to do when you're shorter than everybody else in fourth grade. "Hello? Anybody there?" I asked.

That's when I heard it: a soft, bouncy sound, like a marshmallow dropped on the kitchen floor. I knew there were no marshmallows in the Crypt. Papa said there weren't any dead bodies, either, even though that's what you're supposed to put in a Crypt. Papa said Congress wanted to bury George Washington here, but Martha wanted the President home with her at Mt. Vernon.

But what if George Washington wanted to be buried in the Crypt? What if his ghost had come back to haunt the place? Maybe he waited until all the tourists were gone and the only person left in the Crypt was the girl who forgot where she left her hoodie and he was going to—

That's when I saw it. A ginormous shadow crept up the wall. It was tall and curved, like a ghostly question mark. The shadow quivered in the air. There was a howl, a long, whiny "mrreowow." It seemed to ask,

"Fina Mendoza, what are you doing here?"

"My sweatshirt," I said, my voice cracking.

The ghost mrreowowed again, seeming to echo, "Sweatshirt?"

It was just a stupid school sweatshirt. If it was lost forever, Gabby would yell at me about being irresponsible, and Papa would make me use my birthday money to buy a new one. That was pretty bad, but was it worse than having the ghost of George Washington mad at me? His face looked so serious on the front of a one dollar bill, like he thought I was wasting money on something stupid. Now he wanted to know why I was in the Crypt.

"I'm sorry," I whispered to the ghost. "I'm sorry. I'll just leave now."

Before I could escape, something moved. It was silent. It was swift. Behind the statue of Caesar Rodney, I saw a swish of something black, like a backpack with feet or a garbage bag with a tail. I opened my mouth to scream, but nothing came out. I told my feet to start running, but they weren't listening.

I saw a flash of yellow eyes and the flick of a furry tail. What was it? It wasn't the ghost of George Washington. It was much more real, much more scary.

As quickly as the creature appeared, it was gone.

I unstuck my feet and hurried over to look behind Caesar Rodney's marble boot, just to be sure. What had I just seen? Where did it come from? Where had it gone? Was it real? Or had I imagined the whole thing?

I listened again. This time, I heard squeaky

footsteps, rubber-bottomed shoes on the stone floors.

"Still here, kid?"

It was that Capitol policewoman. The one who yelled at me for not taking off my seven jangly bracelets before walking through the metal detector.

"I–I thought I heard something."

"It's an old building. You hear lots of things," she said.

"Like an animal. An angry creature."

"Ah," she said, and her voice got lower. "The Demon Cat. You have heard of the Demon Cat, haven't you?"

I didn't answer. I hadn't heard of any Demon Cat and didn't want to waste my time listening to some stupid story. Besides, the creature I saw was bigger than a cat. Much bigger.

"The rumor is…"

Oh, boy, I thought. Here it comes.

The policewoman leaned in and whispered. "Occasionally, people will see a black cat that swells to the size of a Mini Cooper, eyes glowing, hissing and spitting."

The creature I saw wasn't quite the size of a small car, but it was black. "Does it yowl?" I didn't mean to ask that, but it just popped out of my mouth. The Capitol policewoman nodded grimly. "It usually makes an appearance right before something really bad happens."

My heart started to beat loudly. I knew that really bad things happened to people. They had happened to me, to the whole Mendoza family, back in California.

Moving to Washington was supposed to get Gabby and me away from all the bad things. I didn't want to think about really bad things right now. My voice got very quiet. "How bad?"

The policewoman shrugged. "Depends. A lawmaker loses an election."

I breathed a sigh of relief. Big deal, I thought. I wasn't a member of Congress. And Papa won his last election by a zillion votes.

"Or bad luck follows you wherever you go," she said, "like the tail of the Demon Cat."

I knew I shouldn't believe her, but I felt a shiver at the top of my neck that traveled down my whole back. The Mendoza family didn't need any more bad luck.

"Or someone could even die," she whispered.

I gasped.

"Beware the curse," she said. "The curse of the Demon Cat of Capitol Hill."

I slowly backed away from her until I got to one of the stone archways. Forget the sweatshirt! I turned and ran down the long, dark hallway to reach the elevator. I could still hear her voice in my head, saying over and over again, "Beware the curse, the curse of the Demon Cat."

"This is important!"

Papa wasn't a very good mind reader. He was still listening to the grumpy congresswoman when his staffer Claudia wandered over to where I was camped out. I remember when I first met her three weeks ago she told me, "I am not a staffer. Staffers are the people who answer phones in the office. I'm a Legislative Analyst. Or L.A." Papa said that meant she was the expert on all the bills that members of Congress wanted to make into laws.

Claudia carried a fat stack of file folders and her yellow notepad. She was always writing on that notepad. "It helps me think," she said.

"Hey, Fina. Nice headband."

I put my hand to my head. It was my sparkly one that looked like a starry night with constellations and everything. "Thanks," I said.

"I wish my hair was long enough for a headband." Claudia had really short hair and really big eyes. She kind of looked like a wise old owl, except she wasn't super old. I thought about owls in a dark forest, which reminded me of the dark Crypt and the swish of black shadows. Maybe Claudia was an expert on more things than just bills.

"Claudia, have you ever heard of the Demon Cat?"

She laughed. "That old story. They drag it out every Halloween. Beware the Demon Cat! The feline that swells to the size of a bus, a sign that bad things are about to happen."

I was going to tell her about the mrreowowing, but

that's when Papa walked over and mussed my curls. It was his way of giving me a hug. "Did you find it, Fina-Finay?" My sweatshirt, he meant. I knew he wasn't too mad at me, since he used my nickname.

"No, Papa," I said. "Not yet."

Papa shook his head. "That's the second sweatshirt you've lost this month."

"It's not lost, Papa. I just haven't found it yet."

Claudia smiled at me and walked away.

"I hope your math is better than your logic," Papa said, and leaned over to look at my homework. He pushed up his glasses with one finger and then pointed to question five. "Missed a step there." He was right. He was always right. My dad was a math whiz when he was in school. Not me.

"Ready to go?"

•   •   •

One of the best things about Washington was walking home with Papa. Walking! We never walked when we lived in Los Angeles. Unless it was just before the election when we "walked precincts," knocking on doors and asking strangers to vote for Papa. But that was more knocking and talking than actual walking. Here in Washington, almost everybody walked almost everywhere, just like Papa and me.

Our house in D.C. was just a few blocks from the Capitol, so Papa and I walked home together every night. It was starting to get chilly. Claudia let me borrow the "office sweater," the one Rules Committee staffers used when the air conditioning was too cold. "Don't lose this one," Papa said. I rolled my eyes and gave him my "hah hah" look. Just because I'm not the most organized person in the Mendoza family doesn't mean I lose everything.

We waited for the signal to change to cross the street. It was the perfect time to ask Papa about the Demon Cat. There were no staffers sticking letters under his nose to sign, no congresswoman shaking her finger at him, no sister Gabby interrupting us. I opened my mouth to ask about the Demon Cat, but Papa started talking first. And not about the Demon Cat.

"Beautiful, isn't it." Papa pointed. I turned around to look at the Capitol building. The round roof they called a dome, glowed brightly under the dark sky. It was so perfectly white, you could see it from an airplane. That's where I saw the U.S. Capitol for the first time, just one month ago as our plane was landing at Reagan National Airport. We were moving three thousand miles away from my best friend Trina in Los Angeles. Three thousand miles away from home.

"There it is!" Papa said that night, pointing out the window of the plane. "There's my office!"

Across the river, I spotted the dome shining in the distance. I elbowed my sister. "Look, Gabby." Her eyes were closed. I heard music leaking out of her oversized headphones. "I don't care. I'm asleep."

Papa rolled his eyes. Gabby was not happy about moving. She started complaining the minute we got the news. "Don't you know this is the most important year of my life!" she told Papa. "I turn 15½ this year!"

Papa had sighed and shrugged his shoulders. "What can I do, mija?"

I thought this was a pretty important year of my life, too. But Papa said it was harder on Gabby because she was in high school. Gabby said high school had nothing to do with it. "Why did we have to move to Washington where nothing happens until you're 16½?" Whatever that meant.

•   •   •

The light turned green. "C'mon, slowpoke," Papa said, picking up his pace as we walked past the gray castle of a building that is the Library of Congress. Now, I told myself. Now was the time to ask. "Papa, have you ever heard of the Demon Cat?"

"Is that a movie you want to see?"

"No. *The* Demon Cat. Of Capitol Hill. It's really, really bad luck."

"Fina," he said. "There's no such thing as a Demon Cat of Capitol Hill."

I knew he would say that.

"Someone's just trying to trick you."

"But Papa–"

That's when Papa's phone rang, and he had to talk to a staffer who worked in his Los Angeles district office. Papa was always on the phone talking to his office, or getting talked to by some voter who was mad about something, or shaking hands with anyone and everyone at a fundraiser. I thought it would be easier to talk to Papa when we lived in the same city seven days a week. It wasn't.

I picked up a perfectly pointed red leaf from the sidewalk and then spotted an almost perfect orange one. A shadow moved, near the pot of chrysanthemums in someone's tiny front yard. The shadow looked familiar. I stopped. Papa didn't notice that I wasn't walking beside him. I crept closer to the flower pot. It was a cat. Not the Demon Cat, but a gray striped cat with big green eyes. He looked at me. I looked at him. "No such thing as a Demon Cat, eh, Fina?" the cat seemed to say, casually licking its paw. "You're sure about that? You already lost your sweatshirt. You want to lose something that's really valuable?"

I shook my head. It was just a cat. It wasn't really talking to me. It couldn't be!

But it was.

"Stay away from the Crypt, Fina Mendoza," said the cat. "If you know what's good for you."

"Fina!" Papa called from down the street. "Ándale! It's getting late."

"Coming, Papa!"

The cat flicked its tail and disappeared into the ivy. But I could swear it said, "Beware the curse. The curse of the Demon Cat."

Chapter Three

Papa found what he called "the perfect Washington house" on A Street SE. SE meant southeast. What a dumb name for a street: A Street SE. Couldn't they come up with more interesting names than alphabet letters? Our street back in Los Angeles was perfectly poetic: Pagoda Place. My mom even planted a miniature Japanese stone tower out in the front garden. "You can't live on Pagoda Place if you don't have a pagoda in the garden, can you?" She always said things like that.

Our new house on the street with the dumb name was a few blocks behind the Supreme Court and the Library of Congress. The brick sidewalks were all bumpy and pushed out of shape by ancient tree roots. The houses didn't look anything like the ones on Pagoda Place. Houses on Capitol Hill were really old and super skinny. Papa called them "row houses." Ours had black iron stairs that made a lot of noise when you clomped up to the blue front door. I don't know why the door was blue. Papa said it was because it was a Democratic house, but I think he was joking.

The house smelled like somebody else lived there. It didn't stink, but it didn't smell like home, either. It was filled with furniture that wasn't ours. Papa said we had to leave our comfy corduroy couch and overstuffed bookcases and even our beds back in California because "it's too expensive to move everything." Papa said we'd move back home to Los Angeles someday. "When the voters get tired of me and elect somebody else." For now, Papa said, it made sense to rent a place in D.C. that was already furnished. In other words, a house filled with somebody else's old furniture.

Tonight, the other people smell in our D.C. house was covered up by something that actually smelled pretty good.

"About time you guys got here. Another ten minutes and everything would be burned!" My sister Gabby waved a wooden spoon at Papa.

"Let me guess…" Papa sniffed. He had a famous nose. My mom used to tell him that he was part bloodhound. That's a dog that sniffs out bad guys. Papa could always sniff out whatever my mom or Abuelita was making. Tonight, he closed his eyes to focus his nose on Gabby's dinner. "Carne asada, steamed summer squash, and…"

Gabby laughed. It was nice to hear her laugh. "You'll never get it," she said.

"Never say never, mija." He sniffed again. "Chocolate pudding!"

He was right again.

Even though we didn't bring our furniture to Washington, we brought just about everything else. The wooden dining room table was still stacked to the ceiling with moving boxes, so we ate in the kitchen. It felt better in there. Not so lonesome, with just the three of us sitting around the table. The fourth kitchen chair was pushed up against the wall under the clock. An empty chair would have been too hard to face every day.

Next week, our grandmother would be sitting in that fourth chair. Abuelita would do the cooking and unpack all of the moving boxes and make our Washington house smell more like home. Last year, Abuelita moved into our house on Pagoda Place. She made sure that we did our homework, signed permission slips for field trips to the La Brea Tar Pits, and stood right behind the dentist, supervising when he took off Gabby's braces. Now, she was coming to live with us here in Washington. "Do you think I'm going to let my granddaughters grow up without me? Besides, your father can't raise you on his own. Washington will be an adventure for us all!"

We weren't supposed to move. When Papa was first elected, he spent weekends with us in Los Angeles and the rest of the week in Washington. My mom flew back east with him once in a while, when she wasn't in the middle of a trial. She told us we'd hate D.C. "Such tiny closets, mijas," she'd say. "Where would you put your clothes? And the ugliest shoes in America!" My mom loved shoes. She had a closet full of impossibly high heels and fancy boots that she wore in court and at least a dozen pairs of fancy flip-flops. One pair was completely covered with fake jewels. "If we moved to D.C.," she said, "I'd have to sell all my beautiful shoes and buy some of those ugly, round-toed flats with a buckle across the front. Yuck!"

So we stayed in Los Angeles with my mom, and Papa flew back and forth every week to Capitol Hill. Until this fall.

Now, all of my mom's beautiful shoes had been packed up and sent off to Goodwill. She'd never have to worry about tiny closets and ugly shoes. Now, Gabby and I were learning how to be Washingtonians, waiting for our grandmother to come live with us in the house with borrowed furniture.

Now, all I had to do was figure out what to do about that Demon Cat.

Chapter Four

Papa licked his spoon. "The pudding was perfection, mija," he said. Gabby smiled. It *was* pretty good. Papa liked chocolate almost as much as I did. I noticed that he didn't mention that the squash was mushy and the carne asada was pretty stringy. My mom used to say that Papa was "always the politician," finding something to praise, leaving the criticism for later.

Papa said, "I'll do dishes, you two hit the homework."

Gabby flew upstairs. I felt the thump thump of her music coming through the ceiling. I guess that meant that she was studying.

"What about you, squirt?" he asked. I still had six vocabulary words to memorize, but they could wait. How could I concentrate on homework when I was facing the curse of the Demon Cat? I collected spoons and forks while Papa tied a towel around his waist. He ran the hot water and scraped the meat bits into the garbage disposal.

"What happens if you lose your election, Papa?" I asked.

"No need to worry about that," he said. "Election day's fourteen months away."

behind all these bald lawyers, and it's hard to see Justice Sotomayor because she sits over near the end. Papa said that's because she's one of the newer justices. Oh, but Abuelita! She wears jangly bracelets just like me!"

"So many things to see, mija. I'll wear my running shoes."

Abuelita didn't run, but she always wore athletic shoes.

"What else?"

I knew she wasn't asking what else there was to see in Washington. She wanted to know what was bouncing around inside my head. Abuelita always knew when something was bothering me. Just like my mom did.

I lowered my voice. I wanted to talk to Abuelita about the Demon Cat, but I didn't want to scare her. Abuelita never read Stephen King novels and refused to go to any movie where things exploded. "I'm a scaredy-cat," she said. "And I don't apologize for that."

Instead, I asked, "Abuelita, do you believe in luck?"

"Por supuesto," she said. Of course. "I am the luckiest woman in the world. I am coming to live with my two beautiful granddaughters in the most important city in America, where my son is the most important man in Congress."

"But Abuelita, do you believe in bad luck? Like a curse?"

"Who is putting a curse on my favorite granddaughter?"

"No one," I said. The Demon Cat wasn't a "someone" exactly.

"Bueno."

"But just in case…" I added.

"Just in case," she said, "cinnamon sticks."

"What?"

"For luck. Put a cinnamon stick in your backpack. That should hold you until I get there. Esta bien?"

"Sí, Abuelita. I love you."

"Te amo aún más." I love you even more.

Chapter Five

Talking to Abuelita made me feel a little bit homesick. In just a few days, my grandmother would be here with us in Washington. But my old school, my old house, and my old best friend Trina would still be back in Los Angeles.

Papa said I could Skype Trina as soon as Gabby got off the computer. Luckily, Gabby had finished her homework and was sitting on the edge of the bathtub, painting her toenails bright blue. She bobbed her head to the music pouring out of the portable speaker balanced on top of the medicine cabinet. I closed the door to the bathroom and grabbed the laptop from her desk. I plopped down on my bed and tapped the icon next to Trina's picture. Trina had been my best friend forever. We lived across the street from each other on Pagoda Place. Moving away from Trina was the second hardest thing I'd ever had to do in my life.

I heard the weird underwater Skype music calling California. It might be getting late here, but I knew Trina was just getting home from school. That's one good thing about living on the East Coast: I can call right after dinner and the sun's still up out west.

"Trina Katrina!"

"Fina!"

It was great to see Trina's freckly face again, even if it was just on the computer screen. She caught me up on all the news–how many times Hunter had been sent to the office and how many times the new teacher had given pop quizzes. She told me who was madly in love with which 6th grade boy and how long she had to stand in line for the new superhero movie. I told her about losing my hoodie. "You should see the ugly uniforms at St. Philip's," I told her. "Blue plaid jumper and white shirts. Every day!"

"Pobrecita. When are you coming back?"

"Papa said we have to stick it out for one whole year. Then, we'll see."

"A whole year!" moaned Trina. "You'll miss everything!"

I know. I already missed Abel Guzman barfing in the middle of class and Backward Day when everybody wore their clothes backward and did stupid stuff like read books from the last page to the first. We talked about Rory, a red-headed boy I had had a crush on last year. By the time I got back to L.A. Rory would have forgotten who I was.

"Trina," I asked, "are you still my best friend?"

"Duh. Of course!" she said. "You're the one who'll forget all about me, meeting all those new important D.C. people. You must have a million new best friends."

"Not exactly," I said. I changed the subject. "Did you ask your mom if you can come visit?"

Trina sighed. "She said it's too expensive. She said

we have to wait to see each other at Thanksgiving."

Thanksgiving. Papa said we would all go back to California over the long Thanksgiving weekend. But that was more than a month away.

"Pixie, stop that!" Trina shouted over her shoulder. "No clawing furniture. You know better than that!"

A cat! I forgot. Trina had a cat. Maybe she knew something about my cat troubles.

"Trina, have you ever heard of the Demon Cat?"

"I own the demon cat."

She was kind of right. Pixie was a one-person cat, and Trina was her person. Every time I came over, that cat gave me dirty looks, squinting its eyes. Pixie even tried to scratch me when I accidentally walked too close to her food bowl. As if I'd want to eat her stinky Seafood Delight. Yuck!

"Trina," I whispered, "I think I saw the Demon Cat of Capitol Hill." I told her about the swish of black and the curse of bad luck.

"Has anything bad happened?" she asked.

"No." Not yet, anyway, I thought to myself.

"Don't step on any cracks in the sidewalk!"

There were beat-up sidewalks all over D.C. It would be impossible to walk anywhere without stepping on a crack.

"You didn't actually see the Demon Cat, did you?" she asked. "Maybe you're not actually cursed. If you stay out of the Crypt, you're safe, right?"

It was the same advice the striped cat gave me on the walk home with Papa. If that cat was actually talking to me. Trina and the cat were right. I didn't have to go into the Crypt. Who cared if there were two Washington Monuments on that National Mall table? There were some mysteries best left unsolved. I would just stay away from that room and never see the Demon Cat again. I would be safe. So would Papa. I felt much better.

"So..." said Trina. I knew what she was going to ask next. And she did. Trina didn't want to know whether I'd met the President's kids or played kickball on the National Mall or seen the cherry blossoms. There was only one thing about Washington D.C. that Trina wanted to know. "Have you seen snow yet?" she asked.

Trina had never seen snow. It was all she asked about, ever since I told her we were moving to D.C. What did it look like? What did snowflakes taste like? Did it crunch when you walk on it? How fast did it melt? "You are so lucky to have snow."

I laughed. "It's way too early for snow here." I felt like I was the expert on D.C. weather, even though we had only lived here for a few weeks.

"You call me the minute it's snowing!" Trina said. "Promise?"

I promised.

Chapter Six

I saw snow up close just once. I was only eight.

It had rained hard for two days. The minute it stopped, my mom threw her pen down on top of a stack of legal papers and said, "That's it." She packed me and Gabby and a bunch of weird stuff into the car. She threw in our old camp stove and a styrofoam bodyboard with a piece broken off. She borrowed gloves from the neighbors and crammed every sweater and jacket we owned into the trunk. The clouds were finally gone, and it had turned into a perfectly sunny Southern California day. When we got off the freeway, she drove us up a scary, curvy road that wound round and round up a mountain.

Gabby usually loved to sit up front in the car, telling my mother how she should be steering with both hands on the wheel and reminding her of the speed limit. That day, as we slowly crept up the side of the mountain, Gabby was almost sick to her stomach. "Why are we here?" she moaned.

"Snow," my mom told us. "Snow."

We climbed higher and higher, looking for signs of the stuff. I was the first to spot the patches of white on the side of the highway. "There it is!" I pointed. "Snow!"

A few curves later, my mom parked the car, and all three of us ran out into a field of white. It was cold and wet and wonderful. I picked up a handful and threw it at Gabby, missing her by a mile. She picked up her own fistful and hit me in the back of my head. It made me laugh. Bits of snow kept melting, dripping icy cold down the back of my neck.

Then my mom did something really embarrassing. She plopped down on her back on a pile of white and started waving her arms and legs like she was doing jumping jacks. Then she got up and pointed. "Look. Snow angel." And there was a perfectly formed angel in the snow.

"Come on!" she said, and grabbed the broken bodyboard. She handed a giant orange plastic disk that looked like a trash can lid to Gabby. We followed her and joined a long line of kids crawling among the trees to the top of a small hill. She sat in the middle of the plastic circle and pushed off, sliding faster and faster down the hillside, until she tumbled into the snow pile at the bottom. We heard her laughing, shouting up at us, "C'mon, chickens!" Gabby and I took turns sliding down all afternoon, screaming and laughing and getting totally soaked.

That first slide was the only one for my mom. She fixed lunch–peanut butter sandwiches and a pot of Abuelita's posole soup that she heated on the camp stove. Mostly, she just sat in the car with the heater running. I could tell that she wasn't feeling good that day. I didn't know then that she hadn't been feeling good for a while, that she would be much sicker in months to come.

It was just the three of us that day on our snow adventure. Papa, of course, was back in Washington, working. When we called him that night, Papa said he didn't mind missing out since he saw enough snow back east, but I knew my mom wished he was here. She missed him. A lot.

The snow on that mountain was old snow. Used snow. Not soft and fluffy like it is on TV. I had never seen fresh, new snow falling from the sky. Papa said that's when snow is magical. The rest of winter, he said, was just slushy piles of dirty old snow stacked up on the curbs. He said winter in Washington was slippery, icy sidewalks, and cold, cold weather that lasted until Easter.

I didn't believe him. Neither did Trina. Snow was magical. There had to be a way for Trina to see for herself. There had to be a way to get Trina to D.C.

Chapter Seven

I asked Gabby for some cinnamon sticks, but she said we just had the sprinkley kind you put on cinnamon toast. I wasn't sure it would work, but I knew we needed some kind of protection from the Demon Cat. I sprinkled half the bottle inside my backpack. I even put a pinch inside Gabby's book bag. I felt safer, but all day at school, every time I opened a textbook, bits of spice flew around my desk.

"Dandruff problem?"

That was Becka. Becka was my least favorite person in Washington. In fact, she was my least favorite thing about Washington, period.

Abuelita warned me. She said starting a new school would be hard. She was right and she was wrong. The hard part was a whole classroom of kids named Jenna and Chloe and Tierra and Mansfield. But no Trina.

The easy part was that my teacher Ms. Greenwood didn't treat me like the new kid by making me stand up and introduce myself to the class or anything like that. She just stuck me in a group to work on vocabulary like I'd been going to St. Philip's since first grade.

Becka announced that she was the group leader before I could even sit down. She bragged that her mother was the chief of staff for a senator, which meant her mom was the boss of his office and since senators were so much more important than congressmen, that meant she was more important than me. I decided to steer clear of Becka. Except that we were stuck in the same small vocabulary group and Becka thought she was in charge.

Becka made it clear she was still the vocabulary boss today. "Valiant," she said, looking around the group, certain that no one but her knew the answer. "Val-ee-ant."

"Someone brave," I said. Like Papa, I thought, when he stood up in front of a room full of people giving a speech. Or like Gabby and me moving all the way across the country.

"I didn't ask you, Miss Fina Mendoza," she barked. "Dusk."

I knew the definition, but I kept my mouth shut. So did everybody else. Becka looked past me and stared at the skinny boy in our circle. "Michael?"

He squirmed in his chair. "The stuff you find under your bed?"

"That's dust, you doofus!"

I was really getting to not like Becka. She was mean as well as snobby.

"Dusk," she read off a flashcard, "the time of day right after sunset."

"Oh," said Michael. "You mean twilight."

That surprised me. Michael might be quiet, but maybe he was way smarter than Becka. Maybe his mom was a bigger deal than somebody who worked for a senator. Maybe his mom worked in the White House. That would shut Becka up.

I didn't even think about the Demon Cat until the end of the day when I picked up my backpack the wrong way, and everything spilled out everywhere. Half a banana, last week's homework and my favorite gel pen went flying. Specks of cinnamon dotted the floor.

"Clumsy," said Becka as she stomped past me, squishing the banana into a piece of paper.

I cleaned up the mess and picked up the–oh, no! Becka had mashed the banana into the picture of my mom. I froze.

"Let me help you." It was Michael. He wiped the picture on his polo shirt and gently handed it back to me.

I looked at the smeared photograph. I couldn't cry. Not here.

"Thank you," I said. He didn't ask about the picture. I was glad. Together we stuffed everything back into the backpack.

"Here," he said. "You forgot this."

Michael held out a small plastic toy. It was a black cat. A black cat with yellow eyes.

"That's not mine," I said.

He shrugged and walked out the door, leaving the cat on Ms. Greenwood's desk.

I walked past the plastic cat. Its eyes seemed to squint at me. I ran out of the classroom.

•   •   •

I caught up with Michael and asked if he wanted to do homework together, but he said his mom was picking him up after school for karate class. Nobody picked me up after school. Papa had signed the "Walk to School Permission Slip" so I was allowed to "walk, bicycle, ride a scooter, or skateboard home unaccompanied by an adult or older student." Back in Los Angeles, Abuelita would walk me to school. But Abuelita wasn't here yet and Gabby had to take two Metro trains to her new high school. So Papa walked me to school every morning and after school, I walked myself to Papa's office. I didn't mind. It was four blocks from St. Philip's to the Cannon building. Papa said Capitol Hill was safer than Fort Knox with Capitol policemen on every corner.

Across the street from Papa's office, there was a dumb little park on top of the parking garage. Hardly anybody used it, except the smokers who can't light up inside the buildings anymore. Today, there was only one smoker and she had a dog. She juggled her cigarette, her phone, and a leash for a ginormous orange pooch. "Hurry up, you stupid mutt," she said. "I've got a ton of emails to get through."

The shaggy orange dog pulled on the leash, interested in something that smelled good over by the concrete bench. The smoker pulled back, still staring at her phone.

"What's her name?" I asked.

She didn't even look up. "Senator Something. She's a he."

"Oh, sorry, Senator," I said.

Senator Something was happy that I apologized. He wagged his tail and danced around in front of me. It was quite the dance.

"Enough. Stop." The staffer was not pleased with Senator Something's dancing.

Senator Something wasn't the first dog I'd seen on Capitol Hill. There were police dogs–German shepherds and black Labradors that patrolled the grounds of the Capitol. But there were also regular civilian pooches who marched up and down the hallways in the congressional office buildings, acting like they were the ones who got elected. Papa said a lawmaker once brought his pet poodle to a press conference, but the dog whined and whimpered and had to be taken out of the room in disgrace.

"What kind is he?" I asked.

"I'd say mutt," said the staffer. "But the boss says he's a Briard. Some French breed that used to herd sheep." The smoker put out her cigarette and tossed it in a trash can. "If the good Senator doesn't get a move on, I'm going to be late for a meeting."

Senator Something wasn't ready to go back inside. Neither was I. It was the last bit of a summery-warm afternoon. Now that the sun was setting earlier and earlier, soon it would be dusk. "Or twilight," I whispered to Senator Something. He barked in approval. His vocabulary was pretty good, too.

Senator Something stuck his nose into a potato chip bag someone had thrown on the ground. He looked funny, such a little bag on the nose of such a big dog.

Big dog! I'll bet a big dog like Senator Something could scare away any stupid cat, demon or not. He would certainly be better protection than cinnamon. If only he was my dog.

The staffer jingled the leash. "Hurry up, Senator Something!"

I had an idea.

"Can I help you?" I asked in my most polite voice. "Maybe let you get to your whatever-it-is you're-going-to-be-late-for and I'll take care of Senator Something."

"You?"

I stood a little taller, the way my mom did in court when she made her arguments to a jury. I tried to make my mouth do the sly smile she used when she pointed out mistakes in the other lawyer's case. "You know," I said, "I'm practically a professional dog walker. Lots of experience. In fact, I used to have my own dog walking company back in California."

I didn't. Not exactly. But I did get paid to feed the Taylor's dog when they went away on vacation for a week last summer.

The staffer finally looked up from her phone. She squinted at me. "You're that California congressman's kid. I've seen you in the Speaker's Lobby during votes." The Speaker's Lobby was another fancy room in the Capitol next to the House Floor. It had paintings of dead congressmen and a real fireplace and big leather chairs to wait in while Papa voted for bills. I sat around in those chairs a lot, waiting for Papa.

"I'm Fina Mendoza," I said. "My father is Congressman Arturo Mendoza from California's 34th district." I stuck out my hand, but hers were full of phone and dog leash. She nodded instead. "I'm completely trustworthy," I added, not mentioning how many sweatshirts I'd lost this month.

The staffer's phone buzzed. She sighed. "Fine. Bring him back to Rayburn 435 when he's finished with his exercise routine. The boss–Congresswoman Mitchell– says he's getting fat and lazy. Kind of like the boss," she added under her breath. She handed me the leash and walked away as fast as her ugly shoes would take her. And then she turned around. "Thanks, Ms. Mendoza."

Ms. Mendoza! So professional. As if *I* was a staffer on the Hill.

"Ms. Mendoza," I said to Senator Something, trying it out to see how it sounded. He tipped his ears back. "You like it, too, Senator?" He barked. I laughed and tugged on the leash to get him to run around a bit. I didn't have a meeting in ten minutes. I had nothing to do except four pages of math homework.

"What do you think about cats, Senator Something?" I asked. Senator Something looked me straight in the eye, surprised, as if he didn't hear me right. Cats?

I nodded. "What do you think about a Demon Cat?" He growled.

"My feelings, exactly," I said.

Chapter Eight

You never knocked on the door of a congressional office. You just walked right on in. That's what I did, holding onto Senator Something's leash. The guy at the front desk was on the phone. Senator Something and I looked around. Congresswoman Mitchell's office was bigger and fancier than Papa's. You could even see the actual Washington Monument out the back window.

Papa said there's a seniority system for everything in Congress, including offices. In other words, the more times you got re-elected, the better your chances of picking out a bigger Capitol Hill office. "Or a room with a view," Papa said. I spotted a photograph on the wall of a young woman shaking hands with President Reagan. He was president a long time before I was born. The young woman in the picture must be Congresswoman Mitchell. I figured she must have a lot of seniority.

Visiting offices was like trick-or-treating. Members of Congress were very proud of the stuff they made or grew in their district, and they were always handing out souvenirs. The congressman from Fresno's office gave out trick-or-treat sized bags of raisins. The congresswoman from Wisconsin's office had packages of string cheese. I kept looking for the office for the congressman from Hershey, Pennsylvania. I figured he probably handed out chocolate. The brass nameplate outside the office said Congresswoman Mitchell was from Georgia. That explained the big barrel of peanuts next to the front desk.

I grabbed a handful of Georgia peanuts, but that was a bad idea. Senator Something thought they were for him. He put his wet nose in my hand and tried to snarf two or three. "No, Senator Something. No!"

The receptionist frowned at me. "Shh!"

Senator Something barked. And then I heard a voice with a funny accent from behind a closed door. "Senator Something!"

The dog's tail started wagging like crazy. I leaned over to take off his leash, but the clasp was tricky. When Senator Something wagged his tail, his whole body shook and wiggled and so did his harness. I sat down on the floor to unclick the clasp. A pair of shiny black high heels appeared in front of me. Senator Something jumped up on a sturdy little woman with fluffy white hair. She wore the round metal pin of a member of Congress on her turquoise jacket. It was the same lawmaker who shook her finger at Papa at the Rules Committee meeting.

"Good boy. Good boy," she said, scratching Senator Something's head.

I didn't know who was happier, the congresswoman or the Senator. They practically rubbed noses. The lawmaker reached into her pocket and pulled out a dog treat. Senator Something immediately sat on his haunches, without anyone telling him to "sit."

"What a good boy," she said.

Senator Something barked again. The receptionist on the phone frowned again. It seemed like the only person in Congresswoman Mitchell's office who really liked this dog was the congresswoman herself. And me. I handed her the leash. "Here you are, ma'am."

You called all the congressmen and senators "sir" here. Unless they're a lady like Congresswoman Mitchell and then you called them "ma'am."

She looked confused. "Do I know you?"

"No, ma'am. I'm Fina Mendoza, Congressman Mendoza's daughter."

She frowned. I guess she was still mad at Papa about not getting a vote for her amendment.

"It's the dog walker, ma'am," called a voice from the back room.

"Ah." Congresswoman Mitchell nodded. "Pleased to meet you, Ms. Mendoza."

There it was again. "Ms. Mendoza." I felt like I was as old as Papa.

She walked back into her office and returned with a five dollar bill. She handed it to me.

"Ma'am?"

"For walking Senator Something," she said. "I can't have you working for me without paying you a salary like everybody else around here."

"Working for you?"

"I'm told you're a professional dog walker. You and

Senator Something appear to be getting along famously. And my staff keeps threatening to call the Ethics Committee if I keep asking them to take the good Senator for his afternoon walk. As if walking a dog is personal business. Is five dollars a day enough?"

I knew I'd have to check with Papa, but I nodded my head. Five dollars a day meant $25 a week. Except most of the time Congress wasn't here five days a week, so it would be more like $20. But $20 a week was a lot of money. I could buy all the raw cookie dough I could eat. I loved those fat rolls of chocolate chip cookie dough, slitting them open and sticking my fingers into the sweet center. The dough tasted much better than cooked cookies. I always wished I had enough money to buy a whole roll and eat it all by myself. Abuelita probably wouldn't let me spend my dog walking money on cookie dough. She'd say to save it for something special. Something boring. Like a new sweatshirt. Or maybe–

I had a brilliant idea. I could save up for an airplane ticket to bring Trina to Washington! I wondered how many weeks of dog walking it would take? Five dollars a day times four days a week times… I decided I'd do the math later.

Plus, I'd have my own canine bodyguard! No Demon Cat would dare bother me now.

"Five dollars a day would be splendid," I said. Splendid was another vocabulary word this week.

"Excellent," she said. "Senator Something will expect to see you tomorrow afternoon. Nice to meet you, Ms. Mendoza. Oh, and be sure to take another handful of peanuts with you. They're from in my district, you know."

•   •   •

I took the basement route to get from Rayburn to Papa's office in the Cannon building. I memorized the way: take the elevator to the Rayburn escalator, up a floor to the Longworth building, then straight down the tunnel to Papa's office in Cannon.

Papa didn't have much seniority. He's only been on Capitol Hill three years, so his office was a tiny space up on the fifth floor. Nobody wanted those offices because most of the elevators only went up to the fourth floor. Just a couple of elevators went all the way up to five. Papa said he didn't mind since he spent most afternoons over in the Rules Committee room in the Capitol, but he felt bad for his staff. Twelve people were smushed together at twelve cubicles, filling up every square inch of floor space. Papa said it was so crowded in there, staffers could hear each other think.

Across the hall from Papa's office, there was a storage room with no nameplate on the door, just the number "87." A black metal cage took up half the storage room, filled with dusty file boxes stacked to the ceiling. The rest of the room was what Papa called my "girl cave." He used it too, for meetings and when he wanted to get away from his crowded Cannon office for a few minutes. But after school, Room 87 was where I hung out to do my homework. It felt like a cave–quiet, with no windows, hidden away from the rest of Capitol Hill, with a slight smell of burnt coffee. There was a TV and a refrigerator and a couch perfect for stretching out on to read history assignments. Perfect, except when the TV set was tuned to C-SPAN, which it almost always was. There was nothing on that channel but a bunch of lawmakers making speeches about something the president did that made them mad. Sometimes they brought big poster boards with pictures of broken bridges or a bunch of numbers. Sometimes they just talked.

I was supposed to be reading about the Piscataway Nation, the Native American tribe that lived in Washington a long time before we moved here and ate a lot of fish and deer and wild plants and grew corn, which they called maize. I wondered why they called it maize.

Then I started wondering about the Demon Cat. Was the Demon Cat to blame for the smushed banana on my mom's picture? What if the Demon Cat wasn't afraid of a dog—even a dog as big as Senator Something? What if Abuelita was wrong about the power of cinnamon? What if bad things started happening again?

Stop it, Fina, I told myself. What do you really know about the Demon Cat?

I heard the door open and the click-click of Claudia's "sensible heels" on the concrete floor. Claudia hated ugly shoes, too. Just like my mom. But I never saw Claudia wear shoes with fake jewels on them.

"You've got orange hair all over your uniform."

Claudia opened a cabinet and handed me a lint roller. Here was another thing I had to remember: dogs have lots of fur, and sometimes it ended up on you. I rolled up and down and told her all about Senator Something.

"Good thing it's not black fur," she said, "or I'd suspect that you were wrestling with the Demon Cat."

She laughed, but I didn't.

Claudia squatted down next to me. "You're still worried about that, huh?"

"Not worried. Exactly."

"You know what Miss Marple would say: the truth can never be as awful as one's imaginings."

I thought about that. Was it all my imagination? What was the truth about the Demon Cat? All I really knew was what that policewoman told me.

"Who's Miss Marple?" I asked. "Does she work on Capitol Hill, too?"

"She's a famous detective," said Claudia.

A detective! A detective got to ask questions without people thinking it was nosy. Like a lawyer. Like my mom.

"Claudia, how does a detective do it? Detect, I mean."

"Hmm," she said. "I don't know any real-life detectives, but on TV they interview witnesses and ask a lot of questions and inspect the scene of the crime, looking for clues."

That's when the vote bells went off.

You could hear them all over the House office buildings: two loud buzzers. They were like the ones at school that told you lunch was over, but these buzzers reminded members that it was time to head over to the Capitol to vote.

"That's my cue to get back to the office," said Claudia, bonking me on the head with the lint roller.

A minute later, Papa poked his head into my girl cave and grabbed his suit jacket from the coat rack. You had to wear a jacket when you were on the floor of the House of Representatives. Those were the rules. Lady lawmakers usually wore lady suits like Congresswoman Mitchell. Ladies weren't allowed to wear dresses without sleeves on the House Floor, even when it was a hundred degrees outside. Unless you were the First Lady. The president's wife got to wear whatever she wanted to wear, sleeves or not.

"Fina-Finay. Wanna come?" Papa asked.

I loved watching Papa stick his plastic card in the voting machine. Sometimes he even let me do it. "Of course!"

"Let's go."

Chapter Nine

"I hear you've made a new friend on the Hill," Papa said as we marched down the steps of the Cannon Building out to Independence Avenue. "I think it was President Truman who said if you want a friend in Washington, get a dog. Sounds like that's just what you did. Congresswoman Mitchell said you were very kind to her canine."

"Papa, she paid me five dollars!"

"That's okay. You only get into trouble around here if you paid her five dollars."

"She offered me a job. Five dollars a day to walk Senator Something after school."

"Senator Something?" he asked.

"That's his name. The dog's name."

"Every day, Fina?"

I started doing the math again in my head. Five dollars a day–maybe by Christmas I'd have enough money to fly Trina out for a visit. She could see real snow for the first time!

Papa must have been thinking of snow, too. "It's going to be really cold walking that dog once winter gets here," he said, making his "doesn't sound like a good idea" face.

I had to convince Papa. I had to walk Senator Something. Not just because of the money, but because he would protect me, protect all of us, from the Demon Cat. I couldn't explain the protection part to Papa, so I tried something else. "I'd be getting lots of exercise with all that walking."

Papa perked up when I mentioned exercise. I hated exercise, getting all sweaty and stinky. I was too short for basketball and too slow for soccer. And I wasn't any good at hitting tennis balls or baseballs. Papa blamed it on crummy hand and eye coordination. I didn't care about sports. I'd rather read a book.

"What about homework?" he asked.

"I can do both. No problem."

"Taking care of a dog is a big responsibility, Fina."

"Just because I misplaced my sweatshirt–"

"Lost it," he corrected. "Twice."

I didn't tell him about the permission slip at the bottom of my backpack that I was supposed to get signed a week ago. "That doesn't mean I'm not responsible. Please, Papa?"

Papa sighed. "Three conditions. One, you check in first thing at my office, right after school. Two, you only walk the dog on Capitol Hill property where the guys in uniform can keep an eye on you." He meant the Capitol Police. "Three, you use your dog walking money to replace your lost sweatshirt."

I was hoping he forgot about the sweatshirt.

"Agreed?" he asked.

That was a word they used a lot in Washington.

"Agreed," I said.

We even shook hands on it.

•   •   •

I wasn't paying too much attention to where we were walking until I noticed Papa heading straight toward the Capitol Crypt. I forgot that he liked to take this route. I forgot about Winston Churchill.

There were statues of famous Americans all over the Capitol, but there was also a metal sculpture of Churchill's head in a tiny alcove just outside the Crypt. Papa liked to touch his bronze nose. "For luck," he said. "We still are masters of our fate. We still are captain of our souls." Papa always repeated that quote by the bald British man before every vote. I thought Winston Churchill must have been a sea captain, but Papa said he was the man who saved England.

Papa touched the lucky nose and kept moving, with me right behind him. And there we were: back in the Capitol Crypt. Papa turned right and headed toward the skinny staircase that led to the second floor.

I froze. This was "the scene of the crime" as Claudia called it. I wasn't sure there was any actual crime. I was sure of one thing: there was something spooky about this room. I shivered.

And then I heard it.

There was the wheezing of the air conditioner, but there was also a banging sound. I looked around the Crypt. Where was it coming from? I looked up. The banging seemed to come from the other side of a grate near the ceiling, the tap, tap, tap of metal on metal. There was something in there, something trying to get out. The Demon Cat! I opened my mouth to scream. Nothing came out.

Papa noticed that I wasn't behind him. "Fina. Where are you? What's wrong?"

"Nothing," I squeaked. "Just looking."

"No time. Gotta vote. Come on."

I ran up the staircase after Papa, telling myself that I was Fina Mendoza, Dog Walker and Lady Detective. The banging wasn't the Demon Cat, trying to escape and curse the Mendozas. The sound was just a beat-up old air conditioner. Nothing to be scared of. Unless I was wrong. Unless–

I started thinking of all the bad things that could happen and shivered. "Stop it, Fina," I told myself.

"Fina!" Papa called.

I hurried after Papa, two steps at a time, all the way up to the House Floor.

•   •   •

Voting in Congress was kind of crazy. First of all, there were no saved seats. You sat wherever you wanted to sit. But all the Democrats bunched together on the left side of the House Floor and the Republicans always sat with other Republicans on the right side of the chamber. Lawmakers called "whips" ran around talking to people in their own party, making sure that they would vote the way their party leaders wanted them to vote. It was the whip's job to keep track of who was voting which way and make sure there were enough votes to pass the bill. Papa said whips had to be very good at math. I told him I'd never be a whip.

While the whips counted and the scoreboard on the back wall counted down the minutes left to vote, lawmakers hung out with their friends, talking in really loud voices about their families or the bumpy flight back to Washington or some new restaurant in town. It was like recess without the jump rope.

Papa handed me his plastic voting card. "Go on," he said. "Put it in the "yes" machine.

"You sure you want to do that?" It was Congresswoman Mitchell.

"Hello, ma'am," I said. Papa smiled to see that I remembered the "ma'am" part.

"You know, Mendoza, they could throw you out of Congress for that, letting someone else cast your ballot for you."

I froze. Had I done something to get Papa fired? Wasn't that one of the curses of the Demon Cat? A politician loses his job?

Papa laughed.

"Carol, you think just because you hired my daughter to walk your dog you can tease her whenever you want?"

Congresswoman Mitchell shook Papa's hand and patted him on the back. There's a lot of back patting here in Washington. I guess she was done being mad at him for not giving her amendment a vote.

"Best dog walker on Capitol Hill," she told Papa. "At least that's what Senator Something says."

"Senator who?" asked Papa. "Oh, the dog."

I smiled and breathed a sigh of relief. Papa wasn't going to get thrown out of Congress.

As Congresswoman Mitchell walked back to her side of the House Floor, I remembered that picture in her office, the one where she was a young congresswoman, standing next to President Reagan. Since she had worked in Washington for such a long time, maybe she knew something about the Demon Cat. Claudia said detectives get to ask witnesses lots of questions.

"Congresswoman Mitchell," I called. "How old are you?"

"What was that?" It was noisy with all the lawmakers talking around us.

I used my outside voice. "I was wondering if you were the oldest person in Congress?"

Suddenly, it got very quiet on the House Floor. Members of Congress stopped talking about extra inning ballgames and what their kid did at the science fair. The whips even stopped counting votes. It seemed like everyone in Congress had stopped everything and turned around to stare at me.

Papa nervously laughed. "Fina, you have better manners than that. Apologize, please."

"But–"

"Fina!" he said.

"Sorry, Congresswoman. Sorry, Papa."

Congresswoman Mitchell harrumphed and walked away. Papa grabbed me by the arm and quickly guided me out of the House chamber. It didn't matter. Everyone kept staring at us until the door swung shut behind us.

•   •   •

Papa didn't say anything more about Congresswoman Mitchell or my question to her on the House Floor. He didn't say anything to me at all on the walk home. Instead, he talked on his fundraising phone, the one he used to ask people for campaign donations. "The worst part of my job," he called it, "asking people to give me money to run for reelection." He was on his second call and he still hadn't said one word to me.

The trees threw long shadows in the "dusk." It really was a nice word. Dusk. I asked Michael why he knew so many words. "Don't tell Becka," he said, "but I like to read the dictionary." He said his mom wanted him to compete in the national spelling bee, but he just liked to collect new words. "Like anise," he said. "It's a spice. Anise," he said, rolling the word around in his mouth. "I'll bet it tastes just like it smells." I tried letting the word roll around in my mouth as I walked with Papa. Anise.

Papa was still on the phone. "I appreciate you taking the time to write that check, Mrs. Alvarez," he said. "You can make it out to the Mendoza Victory Fund. Thank you so much. Goodbye."

Now was the time. I wanted to tell Papa about the tapping behind the grate, about the tingling of the curse. I wanted to tell him the Demon Cat was to blame for making Congresswoman Mitchell mad at me. I wanted to warn him about the disasters to come.

"Papa," I started.

That's when his family phone rang.

It was Tía Catalina. She said my grandmother was at the hospital with a broken leg. I didn't say it out loud, but I knew: it was the curse of the Demon Cat.

Papa hung up with Tía Catalina and called Claudia, asking her to book a flight to Los Angeles as soon as possible. It was a Thursday, and there was one more vote the next day, but Papa wanted to be at Abuelita's side as soon as he could get there. "It's not just her leg," Papa said. "Your grandmother fainted before she fell. The doctors are worried about her heart."

I could tell that Papa was worried, too. Abuelita was his mama. He kept taking his glasses on and off when he talked on the phone, as if he was trying to decide whether on or off helped him think better. He used to do that when he talked to my mom's doctors.

By the time we walked in our blue front door, it was all arranged. Papa told Gabby since she was 15½, she was old enough to be in charge until he got back. He said he'd call just as soon as he had some news. We were to go to school tomorrow as usual and we should call him or Claudia day or night if we had any questions or problems.

And he was gone. Just like that. I was more than a little bit nervous. Gabby had been the boss for overnights when Papa was in Washington and Abuelita was on one of her bus trips. But that was just for one night. How long would Papa be gone? How would we manage alone?

"It'll be fine, Fina," said Gabby. "You and me by ourselves. You'll see."

I wasn't all that sure. I felt the tingling of the curse of the Demon Cat. I knew that our bad luck was just beginning.

Chapter Ten

I had to say this for Gabby: she tried. She got up early the next morning to pack me a lunch and plunked the carton of orange juice on the table. I smelled burning toast.

"Argh!" Gabby grabbed the crispy black slice and threw it into the sink.

"That's okay, Gabby," I said. "I can have a granola bar."

"You need a hot breakfast," she said.

Where did she come up with that? We never had a hot breakfast–at least not since my mom stopped making breakfasts. These days, Papa was always rushing to the office, grabbing a piece of fruit and a cup of coffee as he ran out the door.

Gabby plunked two more pieces of bread in the toaster and pushed down the lever.

"Do you think Abuelita's okay?" I asked.

"I'm sure she is, or Papa would have called us again."

Late last night, Papa called from California. The doctors put Abuelita's leg in a cast, but they were keeping her in the hospital because of her blood pressure. Papa said he didn't know when he was coming back to D.C.

I smelled the toast burning again. "Gabby—"

Gabby used a word that would have gotten her grounded for a week. Again, she tossed the burned toast in the sink. Again, she put two new pieces of bread in the toaster. She stood there watching it, like a cat watching a mouse.

"I thought we had a new toaster," I said.

"It's buried in one of those boxes in the living room. Unless it got lost like all my clothes!"

We couldn't find Gabby's clothes. I found my two boxes of sweaters and sneakers the minute the men started unloading the moving truck. Gabby's boxes were missing. Papa told her not to worry, but Gabby called Abuelita. Abuelita called the movers. The movers apologized and found Gabby's four boxes of clothes in Omaha and promised to get them to her as soon as they could. Gabby was still waiting.

I thought about that mountain of boxes on the dining room table and the stack in front of the living room window, all of them waiting for Abuelita.

"It's gonna be hard for Abuelita to unpack boxes with her leg in a cast." I said.

Gabby and I looked at each other, thinking about all of the things Papa was counting on Abuelita to do for us. How would she walk me to school? Or climb down the stairs to the basement to do the laundry? Or carry groceries back from the store?

"Tell you what," said Gabby. "Let's surprise Papa and Abuelita. Every night, we'll unpack two boxes.

Apiece. Deal?"

"Deal," I told her.

"What time are you coming home after school?"

"I have a dog to walk. So after that."

"You have homework, too," Gabby said. Already she was sounding bossier than Abuelita. "Just be home for dinner. 6:30 on the dot."

"Yes, sir!" I said. I almost saluted.

•   •   •

After school, I dumped my backpack at Papa's office, waved to Claudia, and then hurried over to my new job. The Demon Cat may be sitting around thinking up new curses, but Senator Something needed me to take him out for a walk.

I always wanted a dog. But Gabby had allergies and Papa said "no" so we never had a dog or a cat or a rabbit or even a bird. I had a goldfish once that I won at the church carnival, but it died and we flushed it down the toilet. Now, at last, I had a dog of my own–at least for four afternoons a week.

Senator Something was happy to see me. He wagged his tail so hard it kept hitting the recycling bin. I watched as the smoking staffer fit the complicated harness around his furry chest. "Why doesn't he wear a regular dog collar?" I asked.

"Senator Something has a very sensitive neck," she said. "We think someone abused him before we rescued him at the animal shelter. He doesn't like to have things pulling on his throat, so we use a harness instead of a collar."

I watched as she slipped the contraption over his head and under his belly and clipped the buckle into place. "How did Senator Something get his name?"

She laughed. Maybe she wasn't as unfriendly as she looked. "The congresswoman wanted to name her new dog after a famous senator, so she started thinking about all the famous politicos she admired. But none of them seemed to fit the personality of her dog."

Senator Something seemed to know we were talking about him. He buried his nose in her lap. She scratched the big dog behind his ears and pushed orange hair out of his eyes. "We had to call him something. So we just called him Senator Something until the boss figured out which senator she wanted to name her dog after. That was five years ago."

"Well, he is something," I said. "So Senator Something is the perfect name."

She handed me the leash. "Here you go."

Senator Something was even more excited now. His raggedy orange tail wagged, and he jiggled back and forth. I clicked the leash buckle onto the harness, and we started to walk toward the door.

"Aren't you forgetting something?" She held out a plastic grocery bag. I had no idea what to do with that. "For the poop," she said.

Oh, yeah. The poop. I forgot about that.

•   •   •

Here's the thing about walking dogs: it's more about sniffing than about actual walking. We took a few steps and then Senator Something stopped to check out a patch of grass. We'd walk some more, then he stopped to sniff and think and think some more. I imagined his brain was like some really old computer, trying to find a file buried on the hard drive. Sometimes he found the information in his ancient brain and panted a bit and wagged his tail. Sometimes he just gave up and moved on to the next patch of grass to do some more thinking.

As I was standing around, I started doing some thinking, too. About the Demon Cat. Was it real or just one of Miss Marple's imaginings? What was the truth? What did Claudia say about how a detective worked? Ask questions and look for clues. Asking questions got me in trouble on the House Floor. Where could I find some clues?

Suddenly, my arm was practically yanked from my shoulder. Senator Something took off running like Usain Bolt. He didn't stop until he got to the other side of the park where a concrete fountain was spitting water. Senator Something stuck his entire face in, slurping and lapping up half an ocean of water. I pulled hard, trying to keep him from drinking the other half, but Senator Something was stronger than me.

"It's a matter of grip," said a voice behind me. I turned around to see a roly-poly woman holding six dogs on lots of leashes.

"Are you a professional walker?" I asked.

She laughed. "How can you tell?"

She reached in her pocket and handed me a card. "Dogs on the Hill. Spoiling pets since the Clinton administration."

"Molly Peters," she said.

Wow. A professional dog walker! "Do you mind if I ask you a question, Ms. Peters?"

"Not at all," she said and turned to her pack of dogs. "Stay, MacArthur. Sit, Sgt. Schultz."

I was amazed. Her dogs did *exactly* what she asked. "How did you do that?"

"It's a matter of communicating clearly. Here, watch." She stuck her hand through the round end of the leash so that the loop was on top. She grabbed the business end of the strap connected to the dog. "This gives you control," she said.

I reorganized my grip to match Molly's. Like magic, a slight pull on the leash made Senator Something back away from the fountain. "Thanks!" I told her.

"No problem," she said. "Call me anytime if you have any questions. Gotta go."

Senator Something and I watched as Molly the dog expert and her six canine clients headed down New Jersey Avenue.

If only there was a Demon Cat expert on Capitol Hill.

Chapter Eleven

After dinner, which wasn't even burnt, I shut the door to my room. If there wasn't a Demon Cat expert on Capitol Hill, maybe I would have to become one. As a detective, I needed to start detecting.

I thought about Claudia's old-fashioned yellow notepad. Maybe it would help me think. I didn't have a yellow one, but I found my geography notebook from last year and ripped out the pages with the maps I drew of Greenland and Antarctica. The drawings weren't very good. But there were dozens of blank pages for my Demon Cat notes. On the cover, I wrote in very large letters: D.C. That way, if anyone saw my notebook, they would think I was writing about the District of Columbia, not the Demon Cat.

Gabby was downstairs watching TV. That meant I had the computer all to myself. I typed in "Demon Cat." Lots of pictures of cats with devil horns and pointy tails and bright red eyes popped up. They looked like cartoon cats, not real at all. I searched around online and found out that in the old days, they kept cats in the Capitol tunnels to kill rats. The Demon Cat was supposedly the one cat that never left. I looked at the bottom of the page to see where the information came from and it listed two newspaper articles. Miss Greenwood said it was important to make sure information was from a "reliable source." I wrote it down in my notebook.

Where else could I find information? Hah! It was right there on my desk, the Washington, D.C. tourist guidebook. It was Trina's going away present. Maybe it had some new information. Inside, there were lots of pictures of the Capitol and even the Capitol Crypt, but there nothing about the Demon Cat. I put the book back on my desk.

Maybe I should question an eyewitness. Me. I thought about what I had really seen and heard in the Crypt. What were the details? I closed my eyes and felt the familiar tingling behind my ears. I could almost hear the bouncy marshmallow sound, the whiny howl, the tap, tap, tap of metal on metal. I remembered the flash of yellow eyes and the swish of a tail. I wrote it all in the notebook. Was it really the Demon Cat? Where could it have come from? Even if it was a real ghost, it had to appear from somewhere. But where?

I thought about what Claudia said: detectives inspect the scene of the crime to look for clues. If I was going to be a real detective, I had to go back into the Crypt to see for myself what clues were there. I shivered. I wasn't that brave.

But I knew someone who was.

Chapter Twelve

I explained my plan to Senator Something. "We just need to nose around and look for clues. You're good at that, aren't you?" Senator Something barked in agreement. He stuck his tongue out the side of his open mouth. It looked like he was smiling.

"And if you do a good job," I told him, "I have a special treat for you." I pulled a doggie chew toy out of my pocket. I found it at the gift shop in the basement of the Longworth building. It was shaped like the Washington Monument, but it was made out of plastic and squeaked when you squeezed it. Senator Something knew what it was and immediately wanted to play with it.

"Oh, all right," I said. "Just for a minute." We wrestled for the chew toy, and I held it above his head to make him dance on his hind legs. He caught it every time. "Okay," I said. "That's enough. We have work to do."

After he did his poop business in the park, and after I cleaned it up, we walked over to the Capitol. The plaza was busy with tourists talking in Japanese and German and Spanish. They told their friends to move a little to the left so that they could get a picture with the Capitol dome in the background. One of them even wanted a picture with Senator Something.

We saw another dog on the plaza. A Capitol policeman was walking around with a German Shepherd on a leash. Papa said not to bother police dogs because they were working, but apparently, nobody told Senator Something. He pulled me over toward the K-9 team. "No," I told Senator Something, pulling back on his leash.

"No worries," said the policeman. "We're on a break. Hey there, Senator Something. You want to say hello to Hans?"

I don't know which dog wagged its tail harder. The two dogs sniffed each other. Senator Something even jumped up on Hans' back to try to get him to play. They wrestled around for a minute, pretending to bite an ear or a tail.

"That's enough, Senator Something," I told him, pulling him back. "Hans has work to do." And so do we, I said to myself.

At the door to the Capitol, I flashed my family pass and put my backpack through the X-ray machine. Senator Something's leash set off the metal detector, but the policeman waved us through anyway. We walked past my favorite statue. It was Fr. Damien. I read all about him in religion class because he was a brand new saint. Fr. Damien worked with the lepers of Hawaii. There was even a real lei of flowers around his bronze neck.

Senator Something led the way down the hallway.

When we got to the archway to the Crypt, he stopped. So did I.

It was after five. The visitors were gone. The Crypt was empty, except for a staffer with a backpack over one shoulder who stared at his phone as he walked past us. Senator Something wanted to sniff him, but I held his leash tightly, the way the dog walking lady Molly Peters taught me. The staffer didn't even look up, probably on his way home for the day.

I led Senator Something over to one of the long wooden benches and pulled out my notebook. Bits of spice fell on the floor. I had given myself an extra dusting of cinnamon, just in case.

"Use your five senses, Fina," I told myself. I looked around the room. No sign of the cat. I listened hard. A door slammed somewhere. One of the Capitol policemen at the south entrance laughed. I felt chilly. It was cooler in the Crypt than anywhere else in the Capitol. The bench was hard. I shifted around to try to get more comfortable. Senator Something seemed to sigh and plopped down on the floor. The stones were colder and harder than my bench, but Senator Something didn't care. He stretched out and settled his snout on his paws, resting up for whatever happened next.

There was nothing to taste and no unusual smells. Wait, was that a cigarette? No, not a cigarette, a cigar like the one Tío Tom smoked. I wrote that down in my notebook. You're not supposed to smoke in the Capitol. Cigarettes or cigars. That was an unusual smell.

I remembered a scary movie I watched with Trina. Teenagers in a haunted house kept smelling exotic flowers right before the ghost showed up. Was the Demon Cat a ghost that showed up right after you smelled a cigar?

I didn't think so.

"Enough sitting," I told Senator Something. We slowly walked around the room. Senator Something sniffed carefully at the base of each statue. Satisfied, he led the way through the archway to the Senate side of the Capitol. The fancier side. Curved ceilings were decorated with turquoise diamond shapes and pink circles with gold daisies in the middle. There was a sparkly chandelier, but it was so high up in the ceiling, the hallway was kind of dim. A brass plaque hung on the wall, but it was too dark to read any of the small letters. All you could make out was the name: Samuel F.B. Morse, the inventor of Morse code.

Senator Something started sniffing the floor over by the doorway that led to the old Supreme Court chamber. The floor over here was ancient concrete instead of stones. It was covered with stains and pockmarks and– what was that? There were little marks that looked like– could it be? Paw prints? I got down on my hands and knees for a closer look. Senator Something scrunched down, too. He looked at the floor and then looked at me, as if to say, "Look, Fina! A clue!"

He was right.

There they were! Four little toe dips in the concrete, plus one more for the fat, soft palm of a paw. I ran my fingers over the marks. It had to be a paw print. I looked around. Over by the column, I found another set of prints. And another. Five complete sets of tiny paw prints. I stuck my fingers in the dips. It looked like the footprint of a cat. Here was my first real clue, proof that there were cats in the Capitol! Maybe not now, maybe not the Demon Cat, but cats.

"Good boy, Senator!" I told my canine companion. "You must be part bloodhound." Senator Something wagged his tail. I'm not sure he knew about bloodhounds, the dog that sniffs out bad guys, but he knew that I was saying nice things about him.

I wanted to show the cat prints to Papa, to prove to him that there might be a Demon Cat of Capitol Hill, but Papa was still in California and I didn't have a cell phone camera. Papa said I'd just lose a cell phone like I lose everything else.

Then I remembered that art project we did in second grade to make the kind of autumn leaves they have everywhere in the world except California. The teacher had us stick plain, boring green California leaves under a piece of paper and scribble over the ridges with yellow and red and orange and even purple crayons. Magically, the veins and edges of the leaves appeared in all the colors of the rainbow.

I didn't have crayons in my backpack, but I had a pencil.

Senator Something watched as I tore a piece of paper out of my notebook and laid it on the concrete, covering the paw prints. I lightly ran my pencil back and forth, back and forth. Slowly, those paw prints appeared like magic among the pencil scribblings.

"There it is, Senator Something. Real evidence. Evidence of the Demon Cat."

Senator Something barked.

"Sh!" I said. We both stood still, listening. Senator Something cocked his ears and looked at me. Two seconds later, I heard it, too: the sound of squeaky wheels rolling toward us. I quickly stuffed my paw print rubbing into my notebook and stood up. It was the janitor I saw in the Rules Committee room, the one who put yellow tape in the corners. Today he was pushing a plastic cart with brooms and a mop and in the middle, a big, plastic trash can.

"Evening," he said. "You lost?"

"No, sir," I told him. "Just waiting for my dad, Congressman Mendoza." I pointed to the plastic family pass I wore around my neck. It was almost the truth. I hummed a little bit, rocking back and forth on my sneakers, hoping he'd go away.

It worked. The janitor nodded and rolled his cart past us and down the hallway. I waited until I couldn't hear the squeaky wheels and then got down on my hands and knees to touch the paw prints one last time.

I tugged on Senator Something's leash, to walk back to the House side of the Capitol. As we walked through the Crypt, his floppy ears jumped, bending at an odd angle. We stopped. He looked up toward the ceiling and growled.

There was the bang, bang, banging again, behind the

grate. Senator Something heard it, too! Someone or something was in there, trying to get out!

And then I saw it. A long, skinny shadow crawling across the floor. It was gigantic, the size of the Washington Monument. The real one, not the plastic version. The shadow gradually took the shape of a gigantic cat. The Demon Cat! The shadow was coming out from behind the grate, moving toward me! I froze. As the shadow covered me, I felt that familiar shiver. Was this what the curse felt like? The tingling of disaster to come?

We had to get out of here. I tugged on the leash. Senator Something tugged back, hard. He pulled me over to the display table with the model of the National Mall. He stood up on his hind legs and sniffed the white plastic pieces.

"No, Senator Something."

He whimpered and growled, and then he jumped up on the table. "Down, Senator Something. Get down!"

He ignored me. He sniffed at something in the middle of the table and made a noise in the back of his throat that sounded like a wolf. He stared at the twin Washington Monuments. I heard squeaky footsteps headed our way. "Senator Something! No! That is not your squeaky toy!"

He didn't listen to me. He bit right into one of the Washington Monuments. Senator Something raised his head in triumph, his mouth full of broken plastic monument.

"What are you doing!?" It was that same Capitol

policewoman.

"Nothing," I told her, tugging on the leash, trying to get Senator Something to drop the Monument and get off the table.

"Get down from there! Get down, you stupid dog!"

"He's not stupid," I said. Senator Something shook his head at her as if to say, "No, I'm not. Far from it."

"Get him down. Now! You people think you can do anything you want to do just because you're a member of Congress."

"But I'm not a member–"

"Or the kid of a member of Congress. Or the wife of a congressman. Freshman lawmakers who show up at the X-ray machine without their congressional pins and say, 'How dare you ask me to take off my belt? Don't you know who I am?' Think they walk on water. Treating Capitol police officers like their own personal police department. Do you know what one guy asked me to do? Walk around the block to keep an eye on his wife while she walked their damn dog. There shouldn't be dogs in the Capitol. Or kids of congressmen, either. Get him down. Now!"

"Come on, Senator Something. Come on." I jingled the leash, and he jumped off the table, the Washington Monument still in his mouth. He growled at the policewoman.

The policewoman stared at the display of the National Mall and with one perfect Washington Monument and one broken off at the base. I never did get around to asking Papa why there were two of them.

"Destroying U.S. property," said the policewoman. "You are in so much trouble."

"Drop it," I whispered to the dog. "Drop it, Senator Something."

Senator Something looked at me sadly, then reluctantly dropped the piece of plastic on the ground. The policewoman snatched it up.

"That's it. Take that dog out of here. Now! And don't let me ever catch you here again. Either one of you." She gave a particularly nasty look at Senator Something. "Do you understand me? Wanton destruction of government property."

"But—"

"Your father will hear about this from the OCAS!"

I didn't know what OCAS stood for, but I knew it was something important. And I knew Senator Something and I were in trouble. The curse of the Demon Cat had struck again!

Chapter Thirteen

It was late. Gabby was waiting for me when I walked in the door. "Where were you? I was going to call Papa."

I told her about Senator Something breaking the National Mall model. I told her the OCAS was going to call Papa, and Papa would yell at me, and I didn't even know what the OCAS was. I told her that I would probably get a bill for a million dollars to fix the broken pieces. I told her I didn't have a million dollars. Gabby sighed. She was trying to figure out whether to punish me or give me a hug.

"Come on," she said finally. "We have two boxes apiece to unpack before I figure out what to make for dinner."

Gabby grabbed a box and a pair of scissors and plopped down on the rug. She cut through the packing tape. "Ta-dah!" she said, showing off what was inside. "The new toaster! Your turn." I knew Gabby was trying to make opening boxes fun, trying to distract me from thinking about the broken Washington Monument. How much would it cost to fix it? Papa would make me give all of my dog walking money to the Architect of the Capitol. I'd never have enough money for a plane ticket. Trina would never get to see snow.

"Two boxes apiece. That was our deal," said Gabby.

I threw my backpack on the couch and waded through the ocean of boxes. I picked the smallest one. It was taped up pretty tight. Gabby handed me the scissors. I carefully slit the tape on the top and opened it up. Inside I saw our Christmas manger set. The little shepherds and donkey and wise men were all wrapped in crumpled newspaper, carefully packed inside the wooden stable. Our mom had packed it away two years ago. Last Christmas, we didn't feel much like setting it up. We didn't even decorate a tree.

Gabby was impatient. "What is it?"

I unwrapped a tiny sheep and showed it to Gabby. She opened her mouth to say something. And then she didn't.

•   •   •

That Christmas with our mom was my favorite. It was the first year I was old enough to make tamales. Gabby and my mom and I went over to Tía Catalina's house where the kitchen was turned into a tamale factory: dried corn husks soaking on the stove, the sharp, burnt smell of roasted chilis that would be mixed with pork for the filling, the fistfuls of gooey corn mush, or masa, that you'd spread around on the softened corn husks to make the crust.

The room was crowded with my aunts and older cousins, laughing and telling stories. "Wash your hands, Fina, and come help!" called Tía Catalina.

All afternoon, we'd smear masa and fold corn husks. We'd take home as many as we could carry for dinner on Christmas Eve. Papa figured out who made each one by how much it actually looked like a tamale. Mine looked like a lumpy hot dog.

After dinner, Papa and Mama and Gabby and I bundled up for midnight mass where the choir sang the sweet, sad hymn "Noche Sagrada," or "Oh, Holy Night." As usual, eight million people wanted to talk to Papa outside the church. They all wanted to shake his hand and tell him what was wrong with the country. But that night, instead of talking to everyone about everything, Papa smiled and waved and said, "Feliz Navidad" and we escaped for home and mugs of champurrado, kind of a Mexican hot chocolate, thick with corn masa and smelling of cinnamon. Maybe the cinnamon was there to keep us safe.

It was late and I was sleepy, Papa brought us all out to the front porch to look at the stars and talk to God. He said it was easier to do that out on our porch than in church where babies were crying and the choir was singing too loud. He liked the silence. So did I.

We sat there together, Papa and Gabby and my mom. And me.

"A prayer, Arturo?" said my mom, after a while.

"We thank you, Lord, for our many blessings," Papa said softly. "I ask again for the courage and strength to do the work that the people in this neighborhood need me to do. And please help us to treasure each moment that we have together. Amen."

I remembered that prayer and our Christmas Eve on the porch. I could almost taste Abuelita's cinnamony champurrado and feel my mom squeezing my hand at the end of Papa's prayer. I'm glad I could still remember that night because it was our last Christmas Eve together.

•   •   •

Gabby sighed loudly. She remembered that last Christmas together, too. She wrapped the little lamb up in its newspaper padding and handed it back to me. "Tape up the box, and we'll put it in the hall closet."

Christmas was still two months away. We wouldn't have to think about the box full of memories until December.

It was dark now, and the lamps in the living room made shadows of the boxes stacked on every surface. I was afraid of the other memories taped up tight inside those boxes.

"C'mon," said Gabby.

I followed her into the kitchen.

"Brownies," she said. "We need to make brownies."

Gabby rooted around in the cupboards for unsweetened cocoa and baking powder and sugar and flour. I was surprised. There were actual baking ingredients in our kitchen. "Guess what?" she said. "I figured out how to order groceries online." Gabby was quite proud of herself. "They delivered everything this afternoon. Just don't tell Papa. He'd say that proves we don't need a car in D.C. He's wrong. We do need a car."

We heated the oven and smushed butter all over a pan so that the brownies wouldn't stick. We took turns mixing up the batter and stuck it in the oven. Gabby let me lick the entire bowl. Usually, we fought over the mixing bowl. This time, she just took the wooden mixing spoon for herself. I didn't say anything, but it was covered with way too much batter.

The light in the kitchen was brighter than the living room, and the oven made it toasty warm. In a few minutes, we smelled the chocolate and butter and sugar and flour turning into our favorite thing.

We hadn't had dinner yet and I was suddenly starving. Gabby opened the fridge and plunked a pair of yogurts and a bag of mini carrots down on the table.

"Protein, vegetables. Even Abuelita can't complain about us not eating a healthy dinner. That should leave plenty of room for dessert, don't you think?"

Gabby was actually being nice. Back in Los Angeles, Gabby was usually more crabby than not, but ever since we moved to Washington, she'd been all over the place. Not actually all over the place, like visiting the Jefferson Memorial one minute and climbing the stairs to the Lincoln Memorial the next. She was happy, then sad, then mad, all in the space of about a minute and a half.

I wanted to talk to Abuelita about it, but she wasn't here. And it wasn't something you could about talk with Papa. My mom would know exactly "what was eating" Gabby. But she wasn't here either. All I knew was that the best thing for me to do was stay out of Gabby's way and not give her more things to be mad about. That was harder now that Papa was in California and it was just the two of us. But if Gabby wanted to eat an entire pan of brownies for dinner, that was fine with me.

•   •   •

The phone rang while I was trying to scrub the burned brownie parts off the side of the pan. I grabbed a dishtowel and then the family phone Papa left behind for us.

"Fina-Finay!"

It was Papa. Gabby was upstairs, practicing her clarinet. Before she grabbed the phone away, I needed to hear Papa's voice.

"How is she, Papa? How is Abuelita?"

"Cracking jokes and impatient to come home. You know, Fina, you were named after the right relative."

"Hah, hah," I told Papa. "When does she get out of the hospital?"

"Just as impatient as your grandmother," he said. "Not for another few days. The doctors want to keep an eye on her. How are you guys doing?"

I wanted to tell him about the footprints, warn him that the Demon Cat's curse was so powerful that it reached all the way to California and made Abuelita break her leg. I wanted to tell him to be careful in case he broke his leg. Or worse. I wanted to tell him about the squashed banana on my mom's picture and how Senator Something bit off the Washington Monument. Instead I said, "We're fine, Papa."

Gabby appeared at my elbow. "Lemme talk to him, Fina." She put her hand out for the phone. I sighed. Gabby had a long list of questions for Papa. Should she open the mail? Could she sign that permission slip I kept forgetting to give Papa for my class field trip? Was there any news about her missing boxes of clothes and could she use the credit card to order a new pair of jeans? Finally, she handed the phone back to me. I had one question. "When are you coming back, Papa?"

"After they release your grandmother from the hospital and I get her settled at Tía Catalina's house. I'll be back Tuesday night for votes. But if you guys need me before that, just call, and I'll be on the next plane."

Tuesday night! It was only Friday. I wanted to tell Papa that we did need him now and please fly back tonight. But I knew Abuelita needed him more.

"Tuesday is fine, Papa," I said, trying to sound cheerful. "We're fine."

"I know what you're worried about," said Papa. "Halloween."

Halloween. I forgot Saturday night was Halloween. Papa promised to take me trick-or-treating this year. He said he'd find out which blocks on Capitol Hill had the best candy. But Papa was in California and it looked like Halloween wasn't going to happen at all.

"Not to worry, Fina. Gabby can take you trick-or-treating tomorrow night. Okay?"

"Okay, Papa."

"Oh, and Fina," he said. His voice was more serious now. "I heard about the vandalism in the Crypt."

Vandalism! That was one of our vocabulary words.

It meant "deliberately destroying or damaging property."

"But, Papa," I said, "Senator Something didn't deliberately destroy–"

"I've spoken on the phone with the OCAS–the Office of Congressional Accessibility Services."

That's what OCAS meant.

"It's their table. And they want to talk to you. Monday. Right after school. Okay?"

"By myself?!?"

"If you want, I can call them back and ask them to wait until I get back to Washington and we'll go together."

I thought about that. I didn't want to get yelled at in front of Papa. I didn't want to get yelled at all. But Senator Something was my responsibility and he was the one who chewed off the Washington Monument, so it was my job to take care of it. "That's okay, Papa. I'll talk to them."

"Good," said Papa. "I'm proud of you. You remember where the Hart building is? The Senate office building with the big Calder sculpture?"

I remembered the giant black mountain of metal art in the middle of the lobby.

"The OCAS deputy will meet you there Monday afternoon, 3:30 sharp. We'll talk more about it when I get home. In the meantime, stay out of the Crypt."

After we hung up, Gabby and I looked at each other. We both thought the same thing: a whole weekend without Papa. Anything could happen. Anything.

Chapter Fourteen

I woke up Saturday morning with a knot in my stomach. Would the Office of Congressional Accessibility Services yell at me? Or yell at me and make me pay a million dollars to fix the table? Would Abuelita be okay? What if she was too sick to move to Washington? Who would take care of us? Would Gabby and I have to move back to Los Angeles and live with Tía Catalina? Would we only get to see Papa in August and on weekends? Stop it, Fina.

I needed to do something. I needed to protect Abuelita and the rest of the Mendoza family from more bad luck from the Demon Cat. But how? I needed more facts, and I knew where to find them: the library.

It wasn't hard to talk Gabby into walking me over to the red brick library across Pennsylvania Avenue. "Sure," she said. "I want to do some research about… Never mind." Gabby seemed to have her own secrets these days. She disappeared into the rows of books the minute we walked in the door.

I asked the lady at the reference desk whether there were any books about the Demon Cat. I was worried that she would tell me there's no such thing as the Demon Cat. Instead, she walked me over to the local history section and pulled out a skinny paperback: "Capitol Hill Haunts." It was full of ghost stories, including a chapter about the Demon Cat. The book described the cat as a tabby. In other words, a cat with stripes, like the one I saw on the walk home with Papa. The creature I saw in the Crypt was definitely black. The book quoted a *Washington Post* article that said when the cat looked at you, its eyes had "all the hue and ferocity of a fire engine" and people who saw it were frozen in place. Like me. The book said the cat hadn't appeared in the Capitol for a long time, and that a roller derby team in Washington called itself the D.C. Demon Cats.

Next, the librarian and I waited until the homeless man was done with the computer. She showed me how to read old newspapers online. With just a few clicks, I found it. Right there, in the August 1, 1909 edition of the *Shawnee Daily Herald* from Oklahoma, next to the article about "Amusements for Summer Parties," was a story about "the antics of a very lively cat" and a "most amusing tale."

According to the article, a man who worked in the basement of the Capitol decided to play a practical joke on the policemen who worked up on the second floor. He found a couple of walnuts and "tied the half shells on the four feet of the pet cat."

A pet cat in the Capitol! More proof that there was an actual cat. At least there was an actual cat a hundred years ago.

I thought about tying walnut shells onto a cat's feet. I'll bet that practical joker got pretty scratched up. I kept reading.

Once the guy got the shells on the cat's feet, he turned her loose in Statuary Hall, the big room up on the second floor next to the Rotunda. In the old days, Statuary Hall was the place where members of Congress cast their votes. I guess it was too crowded when America got a bunch of new states and a bunch of new lawmakers. They needed a bigger House Floor.

I kept reading.

"The noise of these shells on the marble floors at midnight, in the semi-darkness as the distracted cat scampered about, trying to get rid of her new shoes, gave the watchers the worst fright of their lives."

I imagined being alone in that big, empty room late at night, hearing the click-clack of walnut shells on the marble floors. I shivered.

"The incident, though a harmless joke, gave rise to the story of the spectral footsteps which follow all those who have to cross the Rotunda to Statuary Hall after the building is closed for the night."

But that was in Statuary Hall. My Demon Cat was on the first floor. And the creature I saw in the Crypt didn't have walnuts on its feet.

I emailed myself a link to the story. And then I looked at the blogs about Capitol Hill suggested by the librarian. One website said that a family of black cats lived here back in George Washington's time when Capitol Hill was called Jenkins Hill. In the 1790's, when workers started building the Capitol, they destroyed the cats' home and scattered the kittens. The blog said that the mama cat has been wandering the Crypt for the last two centuries, looking for her lost babies.

I emailed myself a link to that one, too. Gabby tapped me on the shoulder. "You done?" she asked. She had already checked out a bunch of books and stuffed them in her backpack. I could see part of the title for one of them: "The Essential Guide to Passing Your Dri–" Huh. Maybe Gabby's new school was harder than I thought. She always got A's. Unlike me.

Walking home, I kept thinking about all those lost kittens. What had happened to them once the Capitol was built? Something in my heart hurt for that mama cat, trying for two hundred years to put her family back together. Was that how long it would take for us to feel like we were put back together again as the Mendoza family?

Chapter Fifteen

Gabby said she'd be happy to take me out trick-or-treating, but the way she said it, she didn't sound happy at all. She sounded more like she thought it was something she had to do now that she was the boss. "Don't you have any school friends?" she asked.

School friends. Becka was the opposite of a school friend. Michael might be called a school friend, since he was always nice to me, but Michael was never free to do anything after school that was not on his mom's schedule. Not even on Halloween. His mom was taking him to a corn maze. Trina Skyped me yesterday to show me her zombie costume. But Trina was three thousand miles away. She'd be trick-or-treating three hours after I was already back home counting my candy.

"Never mind," said Gabby. "What about a costume?"

I knew exactly what I wanted to be for Halloween. I had borrowed a black graduation gown from the St. Philip's lost and found box. I wore a white blouse underneath, pulling out the collar, so it showed on top. Gabby helped me poof out my hair, making the curls stick out. I got out every one of my jangly bracelets and put them all on my right wrist. I even found a pair of

Papa's old broken sunglasses, the black framed ones with one lens. I punched out the other lens so they just looked like regular glasses. Then, I stood in front of a mirror and practiced saying "trick-or-treat" in the low, husky voice of Sonia Sotomayor.

I must have done a pretty good job with my costume. When Gabby saw me walking down the stairs, she called me "your honor."

Trick-or-treating wasn't as much fun as it was with Trina back in Los Angeles, but the candy was better. Even the grownups dressed up. People on Capitol Hill really went crazy with decorations, too. There was a Hogwarts house and a body snatcher house. I was too scared to go up to the evil clown house. Gabby said she didn't blame me. We skipped that one.

Gabby said I only had to give her the gummy bears as payment for taking me around the neighborhood. I hate gummy bears.

Afterward, I sat on my bed, sorting my loot into stacks: chocolate, healthy, and everything else. Gabby said I could eat three pieces tonight. I was deciding whether to eat the chocolate ones first or save them for later. The family phone rang.

"You get it," Gabby shouted from her room.

I ran downstairs. "Mendoza residence."

"Fina!" said a familiar voice.

"Abuelita! How are you?"

"Right as rain, mija," she said. She always said weird stuff like that. How was rain right or wrong?

"Except for the giant boot they put on my foot," she

said. "And the fact that I left thirty-five dollars' worth of chips on the table."

Everybody else's grandmother did normal grandmother things—though I'm not sure what those things are exactly. My Abuelita loved to get on the casino bus and ride out to the desert where she played blackjack at the Indian casino. Abuelita loved blackjack. She taught me how to play as soon as I could count the number of clubs on a card. I could add up to 21 faster than anyone in my kindergarten class. Abuelita could play blackjack all day long. And all night long, too.

"That's what happened, mija," she said. "I'd just won another hand and I was so happy, I forgot that I was sitting on one of the tall stools at the blackjack table instead of my dining room chair at home and I fell off and broke my leg. You would think the least the casino could do was to hold onto my chips for me while they took me to the hospital."

"Sorry, Abuelita. But you're home now?"

By home, I meant she was back at Tía Catalina's house, not our old house. That house was rented out to strangers who slept in my old room and stuck their dirty dishes in our dishwasher.

"Sí, sí. Your father came and brought me home from the hospital, and Tía Catalina is taking good care of me."

I heard a voice in the background shout, "You bet I am!" That was my Tía Catalina.

"How are you two doing?" asked Abuelita.

I told her about my job, walking Senator Something on Capitol Hill. I told her about my Halloween costume.

I decided not to tell her about Senator Something destroying the Washington Monument, but I had to warn her about the curse.

"I'm sorry, Abuelita. About your leg," I said. "I should have told you."

"Told me what, mija?"

"I should have told you to be careful, Abuelita. I should have told you about the Demon Cat. Except I never thought the curse would reach you in California. And I didn't want to scare you because I remember how you hate scary books and movies and stuff–"

"Slow down, Fina. What Demon Cat?"

I told her all about the thumping behind the air conditioning grate and the tingling shadow and the research I did at the library. She listened without saying a word.

"You do believe me, don't you Abuelita?"

"Por supuesto," she said. Of course. "I believe that you believe there is a Demon Cat."

I sighed. That was her way of saying, "There's no such thing as a Demon Cat." Just like Papa. Even though Abuelita's leg got broken because of the curse of the Demon Cat.

"Fina? You do have your cinnamon, yes? To keep away any bad luck."

Maybe she did believe in the curse. "Gabby found some in the cupboard," I told her. "The flaky kind."

"Not strong enough, mija. I will send cinnamon sticks back with your father. Much stronger medicine. And how is Gabby? Any calamities?"

"She's—"

I looked around. Gabby was still upstairs. I whispered anyway. "Crabby and bossy."

"Of course she is. She's taking care of *you*!"

Abuelita laughed, and so did I.

"Not to worry, mija. She's not used to being the boss, you know."

"I know."

"And it's not for long. The doctor said I'll be up and around by Thanksgiving."

Thanksgiving. That was weeks away!

"What do you do with an eight and a three?" she asked.

"Double down," I told her. It was one of her favorite questions, Abuelita's famous winning strategy for blackjack. Double down. In blackjack, the best hand was when your cards added up to twenty-one. So if you had an eight and a three, all you needed was a ten. There were lots of tens in a deck of cards. All the cards with pictures of kings and queens and jacks counted as tens, so chances were pretty good that the next card you got would be a ten. Abuelita would double the amount of her bet, or double down. That meant she would get just one more card. Usually, she won.

Double down. That was what I was going to do. I was going to double my efforts to find out more about that Demon Cat. I would work twice as hard to find a way to stop it from haunting us.

Chapter Sixteen

I smelled pancakes the next morning. Gabby was trying hard to make this seem like a regular Sunday. I didn't say anything, even though they were kind of raw in the middle. "Better than Abuelita's," I told her, crossing my fingers under the table.

Sundays we went to mass.

Here in Washington, we went to a different church every week. Papa said we were "church shopping," trying to find a parish that felt like home. Back in Los Angeles, people at Sacred Heart sang songs in Spanish and English, held hands across the center aisle when we sang the "Our Father," and decorated a special altar for Our Lady of Guadalupe.

Nothing felt familiar here in Washington, not even Sunday mass. None of the churches felt like home. We tried out the small stone chapel on the House side of Capitol Hill and the brick one on the Senate side, but Papa said they were too partisan. That meant too political. Democrats went to one church and Republicans went to the other one. Papa said he didn't want to be a politician on Sunday. So we kept looking.

We even tried the "Nat's Mass" at the church near

the baseball stadium where everybody wore red jerseys and caps. But the sermon was always about baseball and Gabby hated baseball. Papa said maybe they would talk about hockey once the playoffs were over, but we kept looking.

This Sunday, Gabby said we'd play hooky. "The weather's too nice to stay inside all day. Let's do our boxes and explore."

Gabby tore open her first box. She grunted. It was the extra toilet paper rolls. Pretty boring. Inside my box, I found a stack of file folders. Some of the papers inside had spilled out. On the top, they said "CA.gov Sample Driver Written Test," with multiple choice bubbles penciled in all over the page.

"Gimme those," Gabby said and grabbed the files out of my hands. She marched upstairs like she was mad at me. I guess we weren't going to explore new neighborhoods today.

Gabby was still upstairs with her precious file folders when I heard the clomping on our iron front steps. I ran to the front window and peeked around the boxes and through the lacy curtains. Maybe it was Papa, coming home early!

It wasn't. It was Claudia, wearing jeans instead of her usual office clothes. I opened the front door before she had the chance to knock. She pulled a binder out of her shoulder bag.

"I brought these for your father to look at when he gets back to town on Tuesday. Proposed amendments to the water bill." She handed me the binder.

"Are you working on a Sunday?" I asked.

"I work every day," she said.

"Really?"

"Not really. I thought I'd see if you guys needed anything. If you were okay without your dad around."

"Did Papa ask you to check up on us?"

"Not exactly. Your dad gets in trouble with the Ethics Committee if he has his staff run personal errands for him. So I dropped by on an official errand." She pointed to the binder of amendments. "Checking in on you guys was my idea."

I didn't care whose idea it was. I was just glad to see Claudia. "Come on in," I told her. "Don't trip on the boxes."

Claudia stared at our mountain of moving boxes. She shook her head. "You guys need to get out of the house for a while. Want to go to the National Zoo? I've got my car."

•   •   •

I was surprised when Gabby said she wanted to go, too. I thought she had to finish reading "Moby Dick" this weekend.

Claudia drove an electric car and Gabby had a hundred and one questions. "Why does it turn itself off at stoplights? Have you ever run out of electricity on the Beltway? Why do they call it a Beltway anyway instead of a freeway?" Gabby seemed happiest when she was talking about cars.

It was our first trip to the zoo. Papa kept promising to take us, but he always seemed to have an appointment or a meeting on Saturday. After mass on Sunday, he usually took a nap.

Claudia took us straight to giant pandas, but there were too many tall people standing around the glass cage. When it was finally our turn in the front row, the pandas didn't do much. They stripped the leaves off long sticks of bamboo and chomped down on the wood. After about one minute, that got really boring. The pandas weren't even pretty. The white part of their fur was more dirty-brown than white.

But there were plenty of other things to see at the zoo. Gabby liked the Reptile Discovery Center with its Gila monster and leopard gecko. She couldn't decide which she liked better: the rat snake from the Everglades or the green anaconda from South America. I didn't like snakes, staring and sticking their tongues out at me. I tried not to look at them. Instead, I kept my eyes focused on the little descriptions underneath the glass boxes.

Claudia bought us hot dogs and potato chips. "Don't tell your father I fed you junk food," she said.

After lunch, we walked over to see the sea lions and the bison and the flamingos. Gabby went back to the snakes.

My favorites were the tigers. The older ones looked angry and bored at the same time. It was clear that they didn't want to be here. I felt kind of sorry for them. But the twin Sumatra cubs, with their big blue eyes and little striped faces, didn't care that they were stuck in a zoo with a bunch of humans watching them. They had a grand time, chasing each other round and round the moat. Those miniature tigers moved just like a cat.

A cat! Like a Demon Cat. I didn't have my notebook with me, but I started making what Papa called "mental notes." I watched the cubs as they stalked each other, pretending the other cub was a wild boar. Then they pounced, wrestling and batting with their paws. When they got tired of that, they hissed and spat as if their brother was a mortal enemy. One minute later, they were friends again, licking each other clean. The whole time, their mom barely opened one eye, just making sure once in a while that they hadn't fallen into the pond. I tried to memorize it all.

"Need a pen?" Claudia pulled a gel pen and one of her yellow notepads from her shoulder bag.

"How did you know?" I asked.

She shrugged her shoulders. "I've worked for your dad for more than a year now. I'm pretty good at figuring out what he wants before he knows he wants it. Must be a family thing."

On the notepad, I wrote:

Cat Behavior:
- Stalking for prey is also playtime for cats.
- Hissing means *stop this now*.
- Cats sleep a lot.

I tore off the page and stuck it in my pocket. "Done,"

I said and handed Claudia the pen.

"Keep it. I've got plenty. Let's see if we can wrestle your sister away from those snakes."

•　　　　　•　　　　　•

The fight started later Sunday night when I dropped a big jar of spaghetti sauce on the kitchen floor. Pieces of glass and red sauce flew everywhere–on the cabinets, all over the black and white tile floor, on my socks. It was a mess.

"What have you done?!?!?!"

I thought Gabby was upstairs in her room, reading her fat book about a boring whale. She wasn't. She was standing in the doorway of the kitchen.

"I was trying to help make dinner."

Spaghetti noodles boiled away on the stove–kind of boiling over, spitting drops of water on the hot surface of the stovetop.

"Don't help!" Gabby said. "And don't move. You'll cut your feet."

"I thought you'd be glad."

"Glad? Glad I have a little sister who throws jars of spaghetti sauce across the kitchen? Glad I moved to Washington, three thousand miles away from my life, my friends, leaving a state where they actually treat you like an adult when you're 15½–"

There it was again. 15½. Why did Gabby think 15½ was such a big deal year? She'd already had her quinceañera on her birthday in April, wearing that big fluffy dress that took up the whole backseat when we drove to church for the ceremony. She let me wear her sparkly tiara at the party in Tía Catalina's backyard. I knew Gabby was sad that our mom wasn't there to see her officially become a grownup. The two of them had been planning her quinceañera forever.

But that was when Gabby turned 15. What was different about 15½?

"How can you be so stupid?" she shouted. "I cook the dinner. I know what I'm doing. You walk your stupid dog and leave me alone."

I started to stomp out of the kitchen.

"Don't move! You'll cut your feet."

Gabby ran to the pantry and came back with two rolls of paper towels. She threw one to me. "Stay there."

She left again. I looked around the kitchen. It was a mess. There were even red spots on the ceiling fan. I heard Gabby open the closet door in the front hall and rattle the empty coat hangers as she rooted around for something. She returned with rain boots.

"Catch."

One at a time, Gabby threw me the orange rubber boots. Then she pulled on Papa's oversized rain boots. A drop of spaghetti sauce dripped from the ceiling fan and landed on her nose. She looked up. Instead of getting mad, Gabby laughed.

"I've heard of raining cats and dogs," she said. "Not spaghetti sauce."

Cats! Was that the reason the jar jumped from my hand? Was the Demon Cat creating small disasters as well as big catastrophes? Catastrophe! Was that what the word meant? Bad things caused by a Demon Cat. What else could that cat be planning for the Mendoza family? And how could I stop it?

Chapter Seventeen

After the spaghetti sauce disaster, Gabby was much less crabby. Especially when we unpacked our two boxes apiece and I found a box of her shoes. It was labeled "mixing bowls" for some reason. Gabby shrieked and kissed me on top of my head, knocking my purpley velvet headband down onto my nose. Then she dragged the whole box of shoes upstairs to her room.

I poked through some of the other boxes, stopping when I came to the one that said "photo albums." I gingerly reached inside and took out the oldest one and sat on a bunch of boxes in the bay window. I slowly turned the pages. There was Papa, speaking at a Labor Day rally, wearing a zip-up jacket and jeans instead of a suit. That was a long time ago when Papa was in charge of the local union that represented the workers who cleaned high rise buildings.

There was a picture of my mom when she was super pregnant with Gabby. Papa was in the picture, pointing at her stomach and laughing.

There were dozens and dozens of pictures of baby Gabby. Sleeping Gabby, Gabby in her crib, Gabby making faces, Gabby crying. Papa and my mom looked really, really happy.

I flipped ahead a few pages. There was me, not so cute, not so many pictures. Papa was out of town when I was born, trying to end a strike and get more money for the workers. I found a picture of Papa standing next to my mom's bed, me a couple of days old. He looked tired. So did my mom. I looked bald.

I skipped ahead. Gabby's First Communion. The Halloween my mom wrapped herself in toilet paper, dressed up like a mummy. The night my dad was elected to Congress.

It was my mom who talked him into running. "It's a once in a lifetime opportunity, Arturo," she told him. "Our congressman dies, and there's an open seat. Look at who else is running. Would any of them make as good a congressman as you?" My mom could make anyone feel like they were the most important and valuable person on earth.

"Why not you, mi amor?" she said. "You spend every election organizing union members to get out the vote. Why not get them out to vote for you?"

My mom promised to take care of "his favorite girls" while he was in Washington. "And you will promise to fly back to California every weekend."

And he did. Papa kept his promise, flying to California every weekend and flying back again. But that meant Papa still missed my Tuesday night soccer games and Gabby's Wednesday night clarinet recital. I know my mom missed Papa every single day, but she would never tell him. "And you must never tell him either, mija," she told me.

I touched the picture of my mom on election night, standing on stage next to Papa, so proud, so happy. He and my mom would Skype every night after we went to bed. She would tell him about her day in court, or laugh with him about some dumb fight I got into with Gabby. Sometimes she would cry. But only after she signed off with Papa. I shut the album.

Chapter Eighteen

We had a pop quiz on Monday. Lucky for me, it was on famous Americans. I got all of the questions right except for the one about Alvin Ailey. I should have gotten that one right, too, since he went to school in Los Angeles and moved to the east coast, just like me. Except he went to New York to make up dances, not to Washington to walk dogs.

Becka told me at recess that she got all of the questions right. Of course she did. Michael said he missed the Alvin Ailey question, too.

I didn't care about the pop quiz. All I cared about was that Papa was coming home tomorrow night. I would make him listen to me. I would show him all of my facts about the curse of the Demon Cat.

But first, I had to meet the people from the Office of Congressional Accessibility Services. The OCAS.

•   •   •

I stood next to the black metal Calder sculpture. The little sign said, "Mountains and Clouds." It kind of looked like a mountain, but I couldn't quite figure out the cloud part. Art was like that. Sometimes you had to be a detective to figure out what the artist was trying to say. I didn't have time for that. I kept thinking of all the ways I would be punished by the OCAS. Stop it, Fina, I told myself. Abuelita would say you're "buying trouble." Stop worrying.

Easy to say, hard to do.

I saw a woman walking toward me, holding a leash with a golden yellow dog. The dog seemed more grown up, more serious than Senator Something. The woman was staring straight ahead, not looking at anything. Of course! She was blind. The yellow dog was a guide dog. He walked the lady straight to me.

"Ms. Mendoza?" the woman with the dog asked. It must be the woman from the OCAS.

"That's me," I said. I wondered how she knew it was me if she couldn't see me?

"Your father described you to me on the phone," she said, as if she could read my mind. "He mentioned you liked to wear a number of rather loud bracelets."

Aha! So that was it.

"I'm Margaret Stevens," she said. "From the OCAS. This is Buster." The dog looked at me, but wasn't interested in what I thought of him. "Shall we go?"

I followed Buster and the lady past the Senate Federal Credit Union office, down a dark hallway where there were a bunch of plastic models of the U.S. Capitol from olden times. Then I saw it: the National Mall display table. My National Mall display table with the two Washington Monuments.

"They fixed it!" I said.

"Actually," she said, "this is a duplicate."

"Why?" I asked.

"Imagine if you came to see Washington, D.C., but you couldn't see? You couldn't read a map. This table is a kind of 3-D map for all of our visitors who are visually impaired." Ms. Burke touched the table. "See? Here's the U.S. Capitol." Her hand traveled down the table. "And here's the greenhouse of the Botanic Garden, and so on."

"But why are there two Washington Monuments?" I asked. The yellow dog looked up at her, as if he had the same question.

"There's two of a lot of things—the Natural History Museum, the Smithsonian Castle. This display was originally built in three parts to allow those in wheelchairs to easily move around it. It took up too much space in the Crypt, so they pushed it together to make one long table."

I looked closer. "But where's the Dr. King Memorial?"

"It's an old display," she said. "Several of the monuments are missing—the Franklin Delano Roosevelt Memorial, the World War II Memorial, the African American Museum..."

"And now, the Washington Monument," I added. "Or at least one of them. I'm sorry. What will all those visually impaled—"

"Impaired," she corrected.

"Visually impaired people do now?" I asked.

"The table will be repaired," she said. "But it will

have to be paid for." She reached in her shoulder bag and pulled out a piece of paper. She handed it to me. "Invoice," it read. "Repair and Replacement of Washington Monument. $360."

Three hundred and sixty dollars! That was so much more than I'd made walking Senator Something. It would take me months to pay for it.

"Thank you," I said, though I wasn't thankful at all. Trina would never see snow. But that was better than all those blind tourists who would never "see" Washington.

"Goodbye, Ms. Burke," I said. "Goodbye, Buster."

Buster gave me a dirty look as he led his mistress away.

•   •   •

It was a long walk to Congresswoman Mitchell's office on the other side of the Capitol. Senator Something was there waiting for me. He seemed kind of impatient. So did the guy answering the phones. "Thought you weren't coming."

"Sorry," I said.

The boy didn't mention the trouble we got into in the Crypt. Even though Senator Something and I were in the doghouse for destroying the National Mall exhibit, I guess no one had told Congresswoman Mitchell. Yet.

Outside, I filled Senator Something in on Buster and Ms. Burke from the OCAS and the $360. Senator

Something seemed a little bit sorry. He was on his best behavior in the park. He didn't try to slurp up the fountain, and he didn't try to escape from the leash. He even played nicely with Bruin, another congressional dog, the shaggy little white pup who wore a blue and yellow UCLA sweater.

After Bruin and his congressman owner left, I told Senator Something that I had a plan. He listened carefully and cocked his head to the side, as if to say, "Are you sure about this, Fina?"

"I am," I said.

Senator Something seemed to think this over in his doggie brain as I walked him back to his office and collected my pay for the past two weeks. Another $40. It was going to take forever to pay for fixing the Washington Monument. But I couldn't worry about that now. I had something more important to worry about: the Demon Cat.

"Goodbye, Senator Something," I said. "Wish me luck!"

Senator Something jumped up on me, as if to say, "Take me with you!"

"No, Senator," I whispered. "I have to do this alone."

I patted him on the head and scratched behind his ears, the way he liked it. "I'll see you tomorrow."

•   •   •

Papa said to stay out of the Crypt, but I had to find a way to stop our bad luck. Splattered spaghetti sauce was one thing, but breaking Abuelita's leg was serious. And what if something happened to Papa or Gabby? Or to me?

The only way to stop the curse was to learn more about the Demon Cat. I needed an expert, someone who knew the Crypt like the back of his hand. I needed a Capitol tour guide.

The only problem: I had to find a way to return to the Crypt incognito. Michael said that means "in disguise." I didn't want that Capitol policewoman to see me in the Crypt. I thought about wearing an eye patch or a wig or pretending that I had a limp. But I figured the best disguise was no disguise at all. I would try to blend in.

I waited in the long line outside the Capitol Visitor Center with all of the tourists. I tucked my family pass in my pocket and went through the security screening like everybody else. Then I looked for school groups. One bunch of kids was taking selfies next to the statue of Helen Keller. They weren't listening to the adult chaperones nagging at them to line up. The grown-ups looked tired and distracted. The kids didn't wear uniforms or matching tee shirts, so it was easy to blend in as long as I kept my raincoat on, covering my school uniform. The kids didn't notice me. They were too busy goofing around, poking each other with souvenir U.S. Capitol erasers. I got in line behind them. I stuck out my hand, like everybody else, and took one of the white tour tickets. I followed the group into the theater and watched the movie about the history of the Capitol and democracy and other stuff. When the lights came up, I followed the kids out to the hallway where a tour guide named Ron tried to get their attention. Ron looked like he'd been giving tours at the Capitol since James Madison was president.

I knew that all tours ended in the Crypt. Eventually. So I just followed along with the group, half listening.

Ron took us up to the second floor Rotunda, where we stood under the dome. Ron told the story of Constantino Brumidi, the artist who fell off the platform where he was painting "William Penn and the Indians" on the ceiling. Maybe the ghosts of Native Americans were mad that he called them Indians. Brumidi had to hold onto the ladder for dear life until someone rescued him.

Ron then marched us over to Statuary Hall, the half-moon shaped room where the cat with walnut shells ran around scaring the guards. The tour guide didn't tell that story. Instead, he made us stand quietly on one side of the room while he whispered from the other side, "Can you hear me?" I rolled my eyes. Claudia had shown Gabby and me the same trick. The curved ceilings carried even a whisper over to the far side of the room. Every kid had to try it. It took a long time. Finally, Ron walked us downstairs into the Crypt.

The Crypt wasn't scary at all when you were surrounded by a bunch of eighth-grade boys making jokes about the funny clothes carved onto the statues.

No shadows were coming from the grate, no "mrreowows" of warning, no swish of black fuzzy tails, no tap-tap-tap.

One thing was different: the table holding the display of the National Mall was gone. Getting fixed, I guessed. I made sure the Capitol policewoman wasn't around to remind everyone who broke it.

When Ron finally stopped talking and asked if we had any questions, I raised my hand. "What can you tell us about the Demon Cat?"

"Demon Cat?" he asked.

"The Demon Cat of Capitol Hill. His paw prints are over there." I pointed over to the Senate side of the Capitol.

"Show me," he said.

I led the guide and two dozen kids over to the hallway by the old Senate Chamber. I got down on my hands and knees and rubbed my fingers over the bumpy floor.

"Here," I said. "Five or six little paw prints."

"Lemme see!" The kids pushed and shoved to get a closer look at the cat prints. Even the tour guide muscled his way in to take a look.

"You're right," he said. "There are paw prints here. You say they belong to who?"

"The Demon Cat of Capitol Hill," I said. I didn't tell him that I'd also seen the cat's shadow. "It's really bad luck," I said. "Bad things happen. Like a grandmother breaking her leg. Or a congressman losing an election. Or…"

"Yes, yes, well let's get back to the tour," our guide said. "Let's not scare the tourists."

"Yes, but what can you tell me about the Demon Cat?" I asked.

"Nothing," he said. "I'm afraid legends and myths are not part of the official tour."

Chapter Nineteen

I could smell it from my bedroom: coffee. Coffee? Only Papa drank coffee. Was he home? I ran downstairs and saw Gabby dragging one of the ugly end tables to the end of the hallway.

"What are you doing?"

"Dia de los Muertos altar," she said.

Dia de los Muertos, Day of the Dead.

Every year, after we'd already stuffed ourselves with trick-or-treat candy, Abuelita would give us little decorated sugar skulls to remind us about the days after Halloween. The first two days of November were All Saints Day and All Souls Day, church days to remember people in heaven and those who had died and were waiting to go to heaven. When I was little, that meant old people like Abuelo, the grandfather who died before I was born.

Abuelita went to mass every November 1st, with a little picture of our grandfather tucked away in her purse. She'd place the faded photograph on a special church altar overflowing with candles and flowers and food and pictures of old people and young people.

Trina's family made their own little altar every year in a corner of the family room with photographs and even a bowl of her great-aunt's favorite food: Ritz crackers. All Gabby and I did for Dia de los Muertos was suck on sugar skulls and think about the next holiday: Thanksgiving.

But one day last November, Abuelita told Gabby and me to be ready to go right after school. "I don't want to get stuck in rush hour traffic," she said. We were going to All Souls Cemetery to visit my mom. Abuelita drove her ancient yellow Lincoln Town Car down the freeway to Long Beach. Gabby sat up front. I was in the back seat. A picnic basket was packed in the trunk. It was our first trip to my mom's grave since the day of the funeral.

Abuelita parked with one wheel on the grass in the back part of the cemetery next to the railroad tracks. My mom loved to travel, and Abuelita picked that spot to bury her because she thought my mom would like to hear the trains go past. We dragged a blanket, the heavy basket, and a beach chair for Abuelita out of the trunk and across the grass to the place where they buried my mom. Mama. I didn't want to look at the marble marker: Grace Herrera Mendoza, "She Changed the World, One Person at a Time."

The other gravestones were decorated with tangerines or a coffee can full of marigolds or sugar-coated sweet bread–pan dulce. One grave for a boy not much older than Gabby had beer bottles stuck upside down in the ground. Bottle caps decorated the edges of the headstone.

Abuelita pulled a stack of baby wipes out of her

purse and handed them to Gabby to clean the dirt from Mama's gravestone. Then she unpacked the basket: roses from Mama's garden, a box of See's candy–just the dark chocolate nuts and chews because Mama didn't think the milk chocolate ones were worth the calories– and of course, that day's *Los Angeles Times*. My mom loved to read the paper first thing in the morning, drinking cup after cup of coffee, hoping to get all the way through to the comics before she had to leave for work. I shouldn't have been surprised when Abuelita uncorked a thermos and poured a cup of coffee. She handed me the mug. I placed it next to the newspaper.

Then Abuelita sat down on the chair and sighed.

"Should we pray or something?" asked Gabby.

We did. And then we were quiet.

I felt the tears in the corners of my eyes. Abuelita gathered me into her lap and let me cry. We never cried when Papa was around. We didn't talk about Mama, either. It was as if Papa might break into little pieces if he thought about Mama being gone.

Gabby blew her nose loudly. That made us all laugh. Then I stopped. It seemed wrong to laugh here.

"No, mijas. Laugh loudly," said Abuelita. "This is why we have come. To celebrate this time with your mom. She is in heaven, sí? So she is happy. And she wants you to be happy, tambièn. She is with us here today, in spirit. But she is with you always." She touched her heart. "In here."

It wasn't a sad afternoon after all. It was our own private party with Mama.

●   ●   ●

"I thought we should make our own Dia de los Muertos altar," said Gabby. "For Mama."

Gabby found a pillowcase with a lot of lace on it and covered the top of the table. It was too late for roses, but she'd cut lots of little chrysanthemums and put them in a tiny vase. I recognized the spiky orange flowers. The lady next door grew them in gigantic pots outside her front door. Gabby also put a *Washington Post* on the altar.

"It's not the *Los Angeles Times*, but oh, well," she said. Gabby opened up the sports section. Even though it wasn't baseball season, she found a story about how the Washington Nationals had hired a Dodger coach. Mama loved the Dodgers.

We didn't have any See's candy, but Gabby put the last brownie on a plate. I knew Papa wouldn't want us lighting candles, so I took the emergency flashlight out of the junk drawer and set it up behind the flowers. It was like a searchlight, shining up the wall, making a little halo over our altar. Finally, Gabby went into the kitchen and brought back a cup of coffee, putting it next to the newspaper.

It was almost perfect. But then I thought about Papa. We never told him about our trip to the cemetery with Abuelita. What would he say if he saw our altar for Mama? Gabby must have known what I was thinking.

"Don't worry," she said. "We'll take it down before Papa comes home."

"Wait," I said.

I found the photo album I'd unpacked from the moving boxes. I flipped through the pages until I found the picture where my mom looked exactly the way I remembered her. She was laughing and clapping, wearing her Dodger jersey, her blue baseball cap a little crooked. I carefully slipped the picture out of the plastic cover and brought it to the altar. Gabby nodded as I placed it right in the middle.

"Welcome to Washington, Mama."

Chapter Twenty

Papa's plane was late getting back to Washington Tuesday afternoon. I'd already walked Senator Something and was puzzling out a page of fractions in my girl cave across from Papa's office when he rushed in, kissed me on the head, and ran downstairs to the tunnel that led to the Capitol. The bells had rung for votes. I'll bet the Capitol policemen didn't yell at Papa for running.

We walked home together in the dark. It was cold enough to zip up my fleece. We crunched through the piles of crayon-colored leaves covering the sidewalk.

"Your Abuelita sent me home with a present," said Papa. He pulled a stick of cinnamon out of his pocket, Abuelita's solution to fighting off the bad luck. "You want to explain?"

I reminded Papa about the curse of the Demon Cat, about the spaghetti sauce explosion and how the Demon Cat was to blame for Abuelita's broken leg. "And Papa, they say if *you* see the cat, you could lose your next election."

Papa laughed. "So the Demon Cat is a political analyst?"

"I'm serious, Papa."

We stopped. Papa leaned over and looked into my eyes. The streetlight made funny shadows on his face. The circles under his eyes were even darker. "Yes. I see that you are serious about this."

"Or you could die, Papa," I whispered.

There. I said it. That was the part of the curse that truly scared me. We lost my mom. I couldn't lose Papa, too.

Papa didn't say a thing, but he hugged me tightly. He smelled like Papa–the familiar breath mints in his jacket pocket and the gooey stuff he put in his hair to keep it from sticking up on TV. Papa unhugged me and put a hand on each of my shoulders. "We're all going to die. Someday, mija. But not now. And not because of a cat, demon or otherwise. Do you understand?"

I nodded. I wanted to believe him.

Papa stood up and took my hand. We walked a block without talking. Then he stopped.

"The House historian!"

"The what?"

"Believe it or not," Papa said, "both the Senate and the House have their own history experts. Go talk to the historian. He knows everything. If there's anybody on Capitol Hill who'd know what to do about the curse of the Demon Cat, it would be the House historian."

•   •   •

Gabby told me she was planning something special for Papa's return. I don't know if "special" was exactly the right word. She decided to try a mole recipe with dark cocoa powder and chicken and bananas. I didn't like bananas very much. I liked them even less when I saw them in Gabby's mole. "They're blue," I said, looking at my bowl.

"Hey, I worked for two hours on this dinner."

Papa gave me his "don't say anything" look. But they *were* blue. The bananas in the mole were as blue as Papa's tie. Gabby looked like she was ready to cry.

"The recipe called for lemon juice," she said. "We didn't have any. I didn't think it was important. How was I supposed to know that's what keeps the bananas from turning blue."

Papa gingerly picked up a piece of blue banana with his fork. He looked at it closely and grinned. "Dodger blue," he said, and popped it into his mouth. "Excelente!"

•   •   •

After dinner, Gabby said she had another surprise. "Fina and I have been unpacking boxes. That's one less thing for Abuelita to worry about when she gets here."

"You girls are my heroes."

"Guess what I found in one of my boxes today?" Gabby pulled out our beat up old Monopoly set. The top hat was missing, and the money was torn and wrinkled, but it was our old game from Los Angeles, the same one Papa said he used when he was a kid. Gabby and I must have played a hundred games of Monopoly every summer.

"Wanna play?" teased Gabby.

"On one condition," said Papa. "I get to be the top dog."

Papa was the dog, I was the battleship. Gabby took the racecar. Gabby won. Winning made her forget all about the blue banana disaster. I just wished she'd stop sticking her hand in my face every time I landed on her green properties, shouting, "Pay up!"

Gabby was like Papa in that way. He loved to win, too. Back when he was a union organizer, he would dance a kind of victory dance in the kitchen every time his union signed a new contract. Abuelita said he danced in the front yard the night my mom said she'd marry him, too. The night he won his election to Congress, Papa didn't dance on the ballroom stage at the fancy hotel where they had the victory party. He didn't dance in our kitchen or our front yard. My mom said it was because he was thinking about all the things he promised to do for the people in our neighborhood when he got to Washington, thinking about what came next.

What came next for us was seeing even less of Papa than when he was traveling for the union. When he came home to Los Angeles on weekends, he didn't really belong to us. There were parades to march in and breakfast meetings to eat at and town halls to go to where every person in the hall seemed to have a complaint about something they didn't like or a problem they wanted him to fix.

"Congressman Mendoza, what about that broken sidewalk on my street?" Papa would explain that it was the city's responsibility to fix the sidewalks, but he'd look into it. And one of Papa's staffers would take the woman's name down and call her back.

"Congressman, I lost my Medicare card, and I've been waiting for more than a month for them to send me a new one."

Papa would promise to make a call and have someone get back to him next week with an update.

I hated those town hall meetings. It seemed like people were mad at my dad, that it was his fault that they were having problems. I didn't like it when he took their problems more seriously than mine or Gabby's or my mom's.

The thing I hated even more than those talky meetings was seeing yard signs all over the neighborhood with somebody else's name on them. How dare they run against my Papa for Congress? My mom warned me, "Don't touch them, Fina. That would be vandalism. They'll put you in jail and wouldn't that be a fine thing for Papa's campaign?" I didn't touch them. But I did spit on them when nobody was looking.

Sometimes, there were special days when Papa belonged only to us. Like tonight, playing Monopoly together.

We packed up the board and the money and the dice and the cards. I noticed that Gabby quietly put the racecar game piece in her pocket. Why? Did she have a secret boyfriend who loved racing cars?

Papa patted the top of the box. "Mijas, I want a rematch!"

Chapter Twenty One

I took Senator Something with me to talk to the House historian. Finding his office, like everything else on Capitol Hill, was confusing. You had to walk through the security screening and then turn around and walk behind the Capitol policemen, then make a quick left turn down a mini hallway. Finally, I knocked on the historian's door.

I expected an old man with a beard. I figured a House historian would be a guy as old as the Capitol itself. This guy looked like he was Gabby's age with Harry Potter glasses and shiny blond hair.

"Yes?"

I introduced him to Senator Something and told him who I was and what I wanted.

"The Demon Cat. No one's asked about that for a while. Have you seen her?"

I looked at his face to see if he was making fun at me. He wasn't.

"I think so," I said.

"So you want to know whether you'll be haunted by bad luck to the end of your days." He walked over to a stuffed bookshelf and pulled out a thick, maroon book. He started flipping pages. "Have you ever been to

Hawaii?"

What did that have to do with my Demon Cat?

He handed me the heavy book and pointed at a picture of a volcano. "There's a strong belief that if you bring bits of lava rock back from Hawaii, the volcano goddess Pele will be angry and you'll be cursed with bad luck until you return the rock."

"Is it true?" I asked.

"People believe it. And lots of people say they've had tons of bad luck–lost luggage, broken engagements, all kinds of calamities–until they return the rocks."

"You're saying I'm having bad luck because I believe the Demon Cat story?"

"Maybe. Maybe not."

I handed him back the book.

"What have you learned so far about the Demon Cat?" he asked.

I told him about the walnut shells and the mama cat story I'd found on the internet. I showed him my pencil sketch of the paw prints. He nodded. He turned to his computer and tapped in a different web address: history.house.gov. He pointed to the webpage.

"Well, the U.S. Capitol Historical Society says back in the 1940's, if you wanted to get a job with the Capitol Police, it helped to have a relative who was on the force. And that meant a lot of not-very-well qualified folks were cops on the Hill in those days. Some of them, shall we say, drank a bit too much. Even on duty. One day, the story goes, one particular guard was taking a nap on duty, and while he was lying down on the floor of the

Crypt, a creature of some sort licked his cheek. He opened his eyes and saw what looked like a gigantic monster."

I finished the rest of the story. "And because he thought he was standing up, he figured the cat was as tall as he was. A giant cat. A Demon Cat!"

It was a great explanation of how a regular cat became the Demon Cat. But it didn't explain what it was that I saw. And it didn't explain my own string of bad luck.

•   •   •

Gabby had been in a prickly mood for days. Even after the moving company finally found her missing clothes. Gabby ripped open the boxes and dumped every single thing on the bed. Her way-too-neat room looked like an earthquake had struck. "I *can't* go out of the house in any of that!"

Everything was kind of crinkly. Sitting around in some warehouse in Omaha, stuffed in boxes for more than two months, Gabby's precious wardrobe looked pretty sad. Even her jeans had creases in all the wrong places. She couldn't press anything because the iron was still missing. We hadn't found it inside any of the packing boxes.

I picked up one of her black sweaters. It wasn't too bad. "What about this?" I asked.

Taking a closer look at the sweater, I noticed a hole near the shoulder and another one on the sleeve. There were little crispy things shaped like rice all along the insides. "What are these?"

Gabby grabbed the sweater from my hands. "Don't touch my stuff!"

"I wasn't touching," I said. "I was looking at all the holes."

Gabby took a closer look. "*My favorite sweater*! What did you do to it?"

"I didn't do anything."

She poked at one of the rice shaped things. A moth flew out. Gabby screamed. I screamed. She threw the sweater down on the bed. More moths escaped. We screamed again.

Papa ran into the room. "What's wrong?"

"Bugs! Eating my clothes!"

"Calm down, mija. I thought the house was on fire."

Gabby picked through the clothes on the bed. There were moth cocoons on the inside of most of them. "They're ruined!"

"I'm sorry, Gabby," said Papa. "We'll take them to the dry cleaners to get rid of the moths and–"

"It's your fault!" Gabby told Papa. "My clothes were fine in L.A. My life was fine in L.A. If we hadn't moved, my clothes wouldn't have been lost in Missouri or Iowa or someplace else in the middle of the country and gotten infested with bugs!"

Papa pressed his lips together. And then his phone buzzed. "We'll talk later," Papa said.

That's when Gabby exploded. "We NEVER talk later," Gabby yelled. "You're a professional talker. You talk to everybody–the President and voters and even Republicans. You never talk to me!"

She was right. Papa always seemed to find time to talk to important people. Not that Gabby and I weren't important. But we were family, not constituents. We couldn't even vote. All of this was spinning around in my head as Papa's phone kept buzzing. Why didn't I say something? Why couldn't I tell Papa that Gabby wasn't just griping as usual? This time, she was telling the truth.

Papa looked like someone had kicked him in the stomach. His face turned white. He turned around and walked out into the hall. Gabby slammed the bedroom door behind him. I could hear Papa telling the person on the phone that he'd call them back later. He hesitated outside the door for about a minute and then I heard him walk downstairs.

I stared at the pile of clothes on Gabby's bed and thought: the Demon Cat wasn't done with us. What was next? And what could I do to stop it?

Chapter Twenty Two

It was getting colder now. I wore a coat over my St. Philip's sweatshirt. I wondered whether Senator Something needed a sweater or a sweatshirt of his own, but he didn't seem to mind. His long, shaggy fur was like an orange, hairy coat. We walked to the smokers' park where Senator Something did his usual poop business. He looked at me and then over at the concrete fountain and whined. He didn't believe me when I told him there was no water. I told him what Papa said, that they turn off the water when it gets cold. Senator Something didn't believe Papa or me. He wanted to see for himself. We walked over and he stuck his head in the empty fountain, and then looked up sadly at me. I tried to explain to Senator Something that it wasn't my fault, that if they left the water in the fountain, it would turn to ice, and crack the fountain and burst the pipes.

Senator Something had another idea. He yanked on the leash and pulled me down the street toward the Botanic Garden where there's a fancy fountain with statues of ladies standing on seashells. Papa said the fountain was built by Bartholdi, the same guy who built the Statue of Liberty.

I tried to tell Senator Something that the water

would be turned off at the Bartholdi Fountain, too, but he wouldn't listen. He kept pulling me forward. My arm started to hurt. I decided to switch the leash to my left hand.

At the very moment I was moving the leash from my right hand to my left, Senator Something pulled really hard. The leash flew into the air, and Senator Something took off running toward the fountain. He ran down the sidewalk, leaped off the curb, and ran out into the middle of the street. He didn't look both ways before crossing. But I did.

I saw a car leaving the Rayburn garage, moving too fast. I saw it turn left onto the street that separated us from the Bartholdi Fountain, the very street where Senator Something was running. The driver of the silver sedan wasn't looking for a big orange dog that dashed out in front of him. He didn't see Senator Something.

I screamed, "Senator Something, no! Stop! No!"

I wanted to cover my eyes, but I couldn't stop watching. Senator Something was at full gallop. The car was headed straight at him. At the very last minute, the driver of the car saw the speeding Senator Something. I heard the squeal of brakes. It was too late.

I heard the thump.

"No, no, no!"

I closed my eyes, wishing it would all go away. Wishing that Senator Something was safely inside his Rayburn office, getting into trouble, eating the peanuts that were meant for visitors. Wishing I could turn back time, wishing I hadn't changed hands with the leash.

But I couldn't.

Please, Lord, I said inside my head. Don't let him die. Don't let him be dead. Please. Please. Please.

I had a terrible thought: the Demon Cat had won. She had finally, truly, forever cursed me. She had won. Senator Something was dead because of me and the curse.

And then I heard a whimper. I opened my eyes. He was alive. Barely.

The car had stopped. The hairy orange pooch was lying in the middle of the street. I ran over to Senator Something. He was panting in little breaths, but he just lay there, not moving. His back leg was bent the wrong way. "Hey, I'm sorry. I didn't see him," said the driver.

I knew him. It was the guy who answered telephones in Congresswoman Mitchell's office. I ignored him. All I could think about was the critter at my feet. I knelt down beside Senator Something. He opened his eyes when I called his name and made little yip-yip sounds. I was afraid to touch him, afraid I would hurt him some more. I didn't want to look at his twisted back leg. I gently patted his head and whispered, "You'll be all right, boy. You'll be all right."

"Oh, wow. How are we going to tell the boss?" asked the driver. "Oh, boy, oh, boy."

That was what he was worried about? Getting in trouble with his boss? It made me mad. We had more important things to worry about. We had to help Senator Something. "We need to get him to the doctor," I told him. The driver looked at me for the first time. I spoke slowly. "Now."

The staffer pulled out his phone and found a veterinarian a few blocks away, over on the Senate side of Capitol Hill. I thought about asking him to call Papa, to have him take Senator Something to the vet. But Papa didn't have a car. And by the time Papa found a taxi, it could be too late. But here was a car right in front of me.

"Open the door and help me lay him on the back seat," I told the staffer.

He put a towel down, and we carefully picked up the big dog. Senator Something whimpered and cried, but didn't resist as we got him into the car. He was breathing hard, his tongue hanging out of his mouth. I crept inside the back with him and sat on the floor. "Hurry," I said.

The staffer climbed back inside and started driving, carefully, slowly. I rubbed Senator Something's head, not even scratching his ears in case it hurt too much. "Hold on, Senator. We're almost there," I whispered.

• • •

I sat in the waiting room, surrounded by cats in carriers and yappy dogs in crates. I still had Senator Something's leash in my hand. The lady doctor had given it to me when she lifted the broken dog onto the silver table. That seemed like hours ago. I practiced over and over again the grip Molly had shown me. If only I had used that grip, Senator Something wouldn't have gotten away. He wouldn't have been hit by the car. The Demon

Cat wouldn't have won.

The driver stood in the corner of the waiting room, calling Congresswoman Mitchell. I asked him to call Papa when he was done. I knew he would do it. Ever since Senator Something got hurt, the staffer had listened to everything I said and did what I asked him to do. I was surprised at myself, barking out orders at someone three times older than me. And yet, he followed my directions. All of them. It was as if I had used my mom's voice. And it worked.

The door to the medical room opened. It was the lady doctor. I held my breath. She smiled.

"He's going to be okay. No running around for a few weeks, no baths. And he'll have to stay overnight."

"Can I see him?" I asked.

I followed the dog doctor into the back, past the cages with sick felines and mama dogs nursing their puppies. In a side room, Senator Something was on the silver table, his right rear leg in a cast. I wondered if it was the same kind Abuelita was wearing for her broken leg. Senator Something was happy to see me, his big floppy tail banging on the metal table. His face looked kind of silly.

"We gave him some painkillers, so he's a little dopey," the doctor said.

"Hey, Senator Something," I whispered, putting my face close to his. "I'm so sorry."

He licked my nose.

"Looks like there's no hard feelings," said the doctor.

"Maybe not from him, but I'm not so sure about his owner," I said.

"You're not the owner?" asked the doctor.

That's when Congresswoman Mitchell burst through the door. "Senator Something! Baby! My poor little pooch!"

Congresswoman Mitchell didn't seem to see me. She only had eyes for her beloved dog. Senator Something was happy to see her, too. The fat tail banged even harder against the table. I quietly backed out the door and returned to the waiting room. Congresswoman Mitchell would never again trust me to walk Senator Something. I made up my mind to give her all the dollars she'd given me so far to pay for Senator Something's veterinary bill. I'd have to figure out a new way to make money to pay for the rest. After I found the money to pay for the broken Washington Monument. I would never have enough money to fly Trina out for a visit. She'd never see snow.

I had an even more painful thought: I'd never get to see Senator Something again. That crazy orange dog had become my friend–my only real friend here in Washington. He was the only one who wasn't too busy to listen to my stories about Becka, to hang out with me after school, to make me laugh. I was going to lose my friend.

I felt the tears coming, but sniffed them back. The door to the hospital part of the building opened again, and Congresswoman Mitchell walked toward me. I took a breath and looked her in the eye. Her mouth was tight.

She looked anything but friendly.

I held out the leash. "I am so sorry, ma'am."

She took Senator Something's leash, without saying a word.

Chapter Twenty Three

Papa didn't say anything either when he came to collect me at the veterinarian's office. He opened his arms for a hug and kissed me on top of my head. A poodle in the waiting room came over to smell Papa's shoes, but he ignored the dog.

"Ready to go, Fina-Finay?" he asked quietly.

I wanted to see Senator Something one more time, but the nurse at the desk said he was sleeping. Congresswoman Mitchell and the staffer had already gone back to Capitol Hill. The staffer nodded at me when they left, but his boss pretended that I wasn't even there. I wished she'd yelled at me, told me how stupid and irresponsible I was, everything I kept telling myself since that leash slipped out of my hand. But she didn't. Instead, I became invisible to her. I shivered again, remembering how cold and all alone that made me feel.

I took Papa's hand, and we walked out the door. We walked past the Italian restaurant and Union Station without saying a word. From time to time, Papa squeezed my hand, his way of telling me he understood. He would wait until I was ready to talk.

It wasn't until we walked past the Supreme Court steps that I spoke. "It was my fault, Papa. I was careless, the way you say I'm always careless. And irresponsible. And Senator Something almost died because of me."

"That's not the story John told me on the phone."

"John?"

"Congresswoman Mitchell's staffer. He feels worse than you do. He knows he was going too fast coming out of the parking garage. He told me how you were the one who took charge after the accident. And that's what it was, Fina. An accident."

"If only I had been holding the leash the way the dog lady showed me–"

"If-onlys will eat you up, Fina. We all make mistakes. It's what we do after our mistakes that shows our character."

Maybe so. But Senator Something was the one with the broken leg. He was the one who almost died. "And I'll never see Senator Something again."

"You don't know that for sure, Fina."

"I saw Congresswoman Mitchell's face when I gave her back the leash. And Papa, it's not the dog walking money. I love Senator Something."

Papa kneeled down on the sidewalk next to me. He whispered in my ear, "I know you do." And then he hugged me, hard. "I know it's selfish," Papa said, "but I'm glad it wasn't you who was hit by that car, Fina." There were little watermarks on Papa's glasses. It wasn't raining. He was crying. Papa never cried. Except about Mama. And now, about me. Papa was worried about me.

"It's okay, Papa," I said. I tried to think of something

that would make him feel better. "The Demon Cat isn't that powerful."

I said it, but I'm not sure I believed it. I just didn't want Papa to worry about me.

Papa brushed away his tears. "You and that cat," he said. "Don't worry. I'll talk to Congresswoman Mitchell."

•   •   •

November seemed to disappear. I even got an 86 on my math test. Becka said she got an 88. I asked Michael if he wanted to kick around a soccer ball after school in the park across from St. Phillip's, but he said he had a violin lesson. Now that I didn't have a dog to walk, my afternoons were empty. Every day after school, I went straight to my girl cave to do my homework by myself. I stayed out of the Crypt.

I thought about Senator Something every single day. I never heard from Congresswoman Mitchell, but John, the staffer, emailed me updates. Senator Something was home from the animal hospital. He wasn't happy about the cast on his leg, but he wasn't in pain either. The Senator was getting lots of attention from all the visitors to the congresswoman's office, and John said even the staff remembered the things they liked about the big orange dog. He said Senator Something was getting so many treats, he probably gained ten pounds already. That was all good news, but I wanted to see him for myself. I missed that raggedy old dog.

Finally, there were just two more days of school until the Thanksgiving holiday. Two more days until we'd head home to California. Two more days until I would see Abuelita and my best and only friend Trina. The Demon Cat had left us alone. So far. But I kept Abuelita's cinnamon stick in my backpack. Was it enough? Papa showed me his cinnamon stick. He said Abuelita made him keep it in his pocket. Gabby refused to put one in her purse. She said she didn't believe in any curse of any old Demon Cat. She couldn't believe I was "stupid enough" to believe it myself. "You probably still believe in the tooth fairy, too," she said.

•   •   •

While Papa cast his last votes for the week, Gabby and I waited in the backseat of a black SUV parked on the plaza outside the House of Representatives. It wasn't Papa's car. Only the big deal members of Congress get cars. But since the Rules Committee chairman was flying out at the same time as us, he offered all of us, Papa and Gabby and me, a ride to the airport.

We weren't the only ones heading home for the holidays. A long line of black SUVs waited with their engines running, ready to take lawmakers to the airport and their home districts. I looked out the smoky colored window and saw a familiar shape in the van across the way. I pushed the button to make the window go down. It was him.

"I'll be right back!" I told Gabby and rushed over to

the other car. Senator Something was sitting in the front seat of Congresswoman Mitchell's black SUV, his head hanging out the window, ready for the long drive home to Georgia.

"Senator Something!"

The orange dog looked up. His whole hairy face lit up like a Christmas tree. He barked with pure joy. He missed me! It had been weeks since I'd seen my best friend, weeks since he'd seen me. He licked my face as I stood outside the van. It felt so good to scratch his head and ears. The driver just nodded at me and went back to playing solitaire on his phone.

"I'm sorry, Senator Something," I whispered to the dog. He stuck his tongue out of his mouth and seemed to laugh, as if he was saying, "No worries. I'm just happy to see you!"

And then he cocked his head, sniffing the air. I looked where he was sniffing. The doors on the second floor of the Capitol flew open. One by one, then in groups of twos and threes, and finally an entire flood of lawmakers streamed out the doors and down the stairs. Votes were over. The Thanksgiving recess had officially begun. Congresswoman Mitchell would be here any minute.

"Goodbye, boy." I patted him on the head. "Be good. I love you." I let him lick me one more time and ran back to our own black SUV.

Inside, Gabby was humming along with her iPod to one happy song after another. Papa had taken all of

Gabby's clothes to the dry cleaners in the basement of the Cannon building. "They'll take care of the moths," he told her. He even let Gabby borrow his credit card to buy a new sweater to replace the black one covered with holes and moth cocoons.

Gabby's good mood continued even when the TSA agent told her to put the "electronic device" in the little plastic tub to go through the X-ray machine. The metal detector beeped again.

"Any coins, anything else metal in your pockets?"

Gabby reached in her jeans and pulled out something small. I couldn't see what it was until it came out the other end of the X-ray machine in the gray bin. It was the Monopoly racecar.

•   •   •

I was excited about flying home to California. Home. Even though Washington was our home now. The minute I stepped outside the terminal at LAX, I sniffed the air, as if I was a dog. It smelled familiar. Drier. And of course, warmer. A lot warmer. L.A. was in the middle of a November heat wave, and I didn't pack shorts or a tee shirt. It was impossible to imagine hot weather when you're living in a place where you had to wear gloves and a jacket every day.

The air may have smelled familiar, but that didn't mean everything was the same. We weren't coming home to our old house. Instead, we were spending the weekend at Tía Catalina's, where I'd bunk with my cousins. The good news was that Tío Tom and Tía Catalina lived just a few blocks from our old neighborhood. Even better news was that they lived just a few blocks from Trina.

Trina was standing outside Tía Catalina's house when our rental car pulled up to the curb. "Trina Katrina!" I screamed as I jumped out of the back seat.

"Fina!"

We hugged and danced a little dance on the lawn. Just like the victory dances Papa did in the kitchen. Just like the dance Senator Something did with his tail wagging every which way the first day I met him. I felt a stone drop in my heart and shook off the fact that I'd lost my best friend in Washington.

But here was my best friend in Los Angeles. My best human friend in the whole entire world. I hugged Trina tighter. Seeing her again made it feel like I really was home.

Chapter Twenty Four

Abuelita couldn't take her usual command post in the kitchen, juggling a hundred and one things to make Thanksgiving dinner for practically a hundred and one Mendozas, but she was still in the middle of it all. She sat at the kitchen table, her broken leg propped up on a chair, ordering tías and cousins around all morning.

"Martha, look at those onion pieces. Más largos! Chop them again, por favor."

"Rinse that bird again. Nothing worse than a dirty turkey."

"You call that a fruit salad? Más naranjas, mucho más!"

She was like General George Washington, heading into battle. All my aunts jumped when General Abuelita gave a command.

Even though this was the 21st century, on Thanksgiving the kitchen was strictly for girls. All of my uncles and boy cousins stood around in the front yard, looking under the hood of Tío Tom's new car, arguing about the kind of car he should have bought. Later, they would take over the family room, staring at the wall-to-wall TV, watching football game after football game. I hated football. And I wasn't all that interested in cars, either. So I stayed in the kitchen.

Not Gabby.

With the heat wave and the oven blasting, all the kitchen windows were wide open. I could hear Gabby outside with the guys, asking Tío Tom how old he was when he got his driver's license. That reminded me of something. Something about Gabby and cars. I thought of the racecar Monopoly piece in her pocket, the pages of multiple choice bubbles filled in all over the sample driving test, the fact that Gabby liked nothing better than to tell someone driving a car how to drive it better…

That's when Abuelita spotted me standing around with nothing to do. "Fina, wash your hands and start peeling those potatoes!"

I didn't mind. Papa was in the back bedroom, on the phone, doing an interview in Spanish with a local radio station. Trina was at her own house, eating turkey. She'd be back later for pie. I dried my hands on a dish towel and found Tía Catalina's old-fashioned peeler in a drawer. I sat on a stool next to a bowl full of raw potatoes and got to work.

It made me happy to be in a warm kitchen with all of these women who loved me and knew my mom. I didn't realize I was waiting for someone to mention Mama until Tía Catalina started telling a story.

"Remember the year Grace left the bag of turkey parts inside the bird?"

Tía Margarita jumped in. "And Arturo thought he was getting a Baby Jesus in his stuffing, as if it was a

Rosca de Reyes cake. But it was only the neck bones!"

Everyone laughed, and so did I. Abuelita noticed that I had stopped scraping potatoes, blinking back tears. She opened her arms and folded me inside. I buried my face in her sweater so my aunts wouldn't see my wet face. Abuelita kissed me on the ear and whispered, "She's right here with us, mija, laughing and telling stories with your tías."

No one in Washington knew my mom, except me and Gabby and Papa and some of his staffers who met her the times she flew out to visit Papa. Nobody in Washington told funny stories about her. And of course, Papa never talked about her at all. But here, in this loud and noisy kitchen, it felt like Mama was here with us once again.

That last Thanksgiving, Mama was too sick from the chemotherapy to help out. She stayed home all day, curled up under the covers. Papa brought her over for dinner and carried her like a baby into the house, all wrapped up in a blanket. She had napped all day to have enough energy to enjoy the meal. She tried hard to tell her own funny stories as she passed the stuffing and praised the gravy. I noticed that she only ate a bite or two of anything on her plate. She was ready to go home before the pies were cut for dessert.

A loud burst of laughter from the tías interrupted my thoughts.

"Remember the time Grace used tofu instead of milk and eggs in her pumpkin pie? And the only one who would eat it was Tío Tom because he eats anything!"

They laughed again. I laughed, too. Abuelita kissed me on top of my head and pushed me back toward the pile of potatoes.

•   •   •

The Mendoza family Thanksgiving was always a little crazy. There were dozens of cousins sitting on folding chairs, milk crates, even a stepstool. The table was packed with food like Tía Catalina's weird stuffing that always had way too many chili peppers in it. Alongside the turkey and the mashed potatoes and the gravy, there were tamales. There were always tamales. And if you didn't like pumpkin pie, there was postre de limon for dessert.

Later, while the boys watched football in the TV room, the girls took over the rest of the house for a different annual tradition: the Mendoza family clothes swap.

My mom said it started when all the cousins were babies, outgrowing clothes faster than the tías could buy them. On Thanksgiving, all the moms brought a bag of kids' clothes to pass on to younger cousins. You would always see the same reindeer sweater or red velvet dress on a different cousin in everybody's Mendoza family Christmas picture.

I didn't mind wearing "upcycled fashion" as my mom used to call it. I didn't like shopping in stores with those ugly dressing rooms where the sales lady barged in when you were still in your underwear to ask if anything fit. Nothing ever fit.

The Mendoza clothing swap involved more than Mendozas now. It had grown over the years into this gigantic neighborhood event. Dozens of moms and old ladies and kids of every size crowded into Tía Catalina's living room, which was turned into the Mendoza boutique. Clothes of every kind were stacked everywhere. There were sweaters on the piano, skirts on the sofa, pants on the armchair, dresses hanging from the bookcase. Shoes took up an entire corner. There were belts and jewelry and even a hat or two. It was like shopping at a private sale. "A trunk show," Tía Catalina described it. Except it was free.

Usually, Gabby took a quick tour, grabbed a tee shirt, and took off to hang out with her friends. This year, she tried on everything. "All my jeans have wrinkles in their wrinkles, and everything else is lunch for moths," she told her cousins. "And you should see what they sell in the stores in D.C. Black and gray and boring! I need some California style."

"You sound like your mom," said Tía Catalina.

Trina brought two bags of stuff with her, and we sorted it out. Pink cowboy boots, a leather biker jacket that was too small for her, and a fancy party dress with ruffles that she'd worn just once. "I almost brought this excellent pair of pink striped tights, but Pixie clawed them and snagged them."

Pixie! Trina's stupid cat. "Why did Pixie claw up your tights?" I asked, "Was she mad at you?"

"Nah. Pixie gets bored when I'm at school, and there

was one leg of my tights hanging out of the drawer. She probably was playing with it like she does with her sparkle bird toy."

Was the Demon Cat playing with us? Did she think it was fun to curse us with bad luck? Was there a way to distract her, so that she would stop treating us like a sparkle toy?

"What about the curse?" Trina asked. "Anything else bad happen?"

Well, there was the moth invasion of Gabby's sweaters, but I wasn't sure that could be blamed on the Demon Cat.

"So far, so good," I told her. All the bad luck of the Demon Cat seemed to stay back in Washington. Maybe D.C.–the Demon Cat–could only cause trouble in D.C.– the District of Columbia. But then I remembered Abuelita's broken leg. That didn't happen in Washington.

Just to be sure, I grabbed a handful of fresh cinnamon sticks from Tía Caroline's spice rack and stuck them in all my pockets. So far, so good.

I had a funny feeling in my stomach anyway.

Chapter Twenty Five

All Thanksgiving weekend, I talked to tías and uncles, cousins and neighbors. I talked to all of Abuelita's old lady friends who came over to visit.

The one person I didn't talk to was Papa. He was busy talking to his brothers and his sisters and his nieces and nephews and all of his constituents. From time to time, I'd stand near Papa and occasionally, he'd muss my hair to let me know that he knew I was there. But there were too many people around for him to talk just to me.

On Saturday, Papa was in a Christmas parade. So were we! It was another bright sunny California day. Gabby and I wore sunglasses and sat in the back seat of an old-fashioned convertible. There was a paper sign on the side of the baby blue Cadillac that read "Congressman Arturo Mendoza." Papa sat in the front seat, waving to the people on the sidewalk. It was exciting, but also kind of embarrassing and dumb. Gabby and I decided to practice our queen wave, pointing our fingers straight up and twisting our hands back and forth, like the Queen of the Rose Parade.

Gabby was really interested in the car. She asked the man driving us what year the Cadillac was made, was it hard to shift gears when they're next to the steering wheel instead of on the floor, what was the secret to parallel parking a car that big? Papa told her to be quiet and let the man drive.

After the parade, Gabby wanted to see her L.A. friends. I went with Papa to visit veterans at a hall. It was dark inside and smelled like burned popcorn. Some of the soldiers were really old, but most were younger guys. There were even a few women who had served in Afghanistan. Papa sat on a cold metal folding chair in a circle with them. He thanked them for their service and asked what he could do for them. They had a long list.

"Congressman Mendoza, why does it take so long to get an appointment at the V.A. hospital?"

"Why does the community college keep losing my paperwork for financial aid?"

"Why is it so hard to find a job?"

As usual, a staffer who worked in Papa's L.A. office took notes. As usual, Papa promised to follow up with each and every veteran. It made me sad, listening to their stories. I think Papa was sad, too. It seemed like all their troubles made Papa's shoulders slump a little.

On our way back to Tía Catalina's, Papa turned left and drove down Pagoda Place. He stopped the car in front of our old house. We sat there for a minute, not saying anything. The house looked the same, but different. There were toys for little kids out on the front lawn–a plastic dump truck, a soccer ball that was practically flat, a pink plastic tricycle. It made my heart hurt to see pieces of another family's life crowding out memories of our family living there, memories of my mom. I didn't want to see our old life erased by somebody else, our old house turned into someone else's home. "Can we go?" I asked.

Papa kept staring at the rose bushes my mom had planted in every shade of pink, at the dented mailbox my mom had hit with the car as she was backing out of the driveway one morning when we were late for school, at the windows where my mom's face would never again peek out and wave to Papa as he climbed into the taxi that would take him to the airport for his flight back to Washington.

"Papa?"

Papa took his handkerchief out of his pocket and blew his nose. Hard. He squeezed his eyes together, to trap all the tears inside.

"I miss her, too, Papa," I said softly. "Every day."

Papa took a deep breath and let it out. He leaned over and kissed me on top of my head. And then he started the car.

Chapter Twenty Six

I knew something was up the minute we got back to Tía Catalina's house. Tío Tom's new car was in the driveway. Its back bumper was crumpled on one side. Abuelita was sitting on the front porch swing, her broken leg resting on an upside down flower pot. "Now, Arturo, don't be mad," she said.

"Mad? About what?"

Papa hadn't noticed the bumper. I don't think he even noticed that Tío Tom had a new car.

"Talk to your daughter," said Abuelita. "And don't overreact."

Papa put on his "I don't need this right now" face and opened the screen door. Abuelita put her finger to her lips to remind me to keep my mouth shut. I followed Papa inside.

Gabby was sitting on the sofa, waiting, worried. She immediately stood up when Papa came into the living room. "It was an accident," said Gabby. "I didn't see the little gate in the parking lot when I was backing up…"

Papa's face went white. He looked the way he did when he told me he was worried that it was me, not Senator Something who got hit by the car.

"Are you all right?" he asked.

"I'm fine," Gabby said.

Papa seemed relieved. And then he wasn't. "Wait a minute. Wait a minute. What do you mean 'when you were backing up?' You were driving? What were you doing behind the wheel of a car?"

"Tío Tom was giving me a driving lesson and–"

"You don't have a learner's permit," said Papa.

"And whose fault is that?" she shouted. "Yours! If I was still living in Los Angeles, I would be four weeks into driver's education classes. I was supposed to start this fall! I'm 15½! Old enough to take drivers ed and get my learner's permit. I would have my driver's license by Memorial Day. I could drive to the beach all summer or go shopping at the mall or even take Abuelita to her doctor appointments. I could be a normal California person who drives everywhere. But no, you move us a million miles to stupid Washington, D.C. where they don't give learner's permits until you're 16½. 16½! That's a whole year away! Instead, I have to take the stupid, stinky Red Line every day to school, stuffed with tourists who don't know where they're going, and they're always on the wrong train, and you have to give them directions and there's these women with baby strollers bigger than Tío Tom's car that bang into your leg every time the trains stops and do you know how many times there's a 'delay on the Red Line and Metro apologizes for the inconvenience', and it's always when the air conditioning isn't working and I'm stuck there with all these sweaty people…"

That was it. That was what was bugging Gabby. It

wasn't homesickness or school. The thing she missed most about California was cars. She wanted to drive, and she didn't want to wait a whole year to do it. It all made sense now.

I went outside to the porch and sat next to Abuelita on the swing. "No yelling from your father. That's good," she said.

"I solved one mystery," I said. "Why Gabby's been so crabby. She just wanted to learn how to drive."

That was a relief. And then it wasn't. I thought about Gabby's accident. I was wrong. The curse of the Demon Cat did reach outside of Washington. That darned cat! It broke Abuelita's leg. It caused Gabby's accident in Tío Tom's car. It almost killed Senator Something. The only person not yet touched by the curse of the Demon Cat was Papa. Papa!

Now I was really worried. It must have shown in my face because Abuelita asked, "What's wrong, mija?"

"The cinnamon sticks stopped working."

I told her about the Demon Cat, about the exploding spaghetti sauce and Senator Something breaking his leg, and now, Gabby's accident.

"And now you fear the bad luck will stick to your father." She straightened my headband of curly orange ribbons and held my hand next to her heart. "Yo comprendo. It is a terrible thing to lose your mother. I was practically an old lady when mi madre died. You're still a baby."

"I'm not a baby, Abuelita."

"No, of course you're not. But in your heart, you

secretly fear that you might also lose your father. That he might die as well."

That's when I cried, my head in Abuelita's lap, feeling like the baby she called me. I was afraid for Papa and missed my mom. Even when she was mad at me for not picking up my socks or forgetting to do my math homework, I knew that she loved me. I could have told her about stupid stuck up Becka, about the Capitol policewoman who was so mean and scary. She would have figured out Gabby's craziness about cars. She would probably even find the Demon Cat and tell it a thing or two.

"You are like her, you know," said Abuelita. "Fearless. Funny. Kind. Smart as the devil. You go back to Washington tomorrow, and you confront that cursed cat."

"But the cinnamon—"

She reached into her pocket. "You need something stronger than cinnamon, mi amor."

She took out a torn playing card. The queen of hearts. She kissed it and pressed it into my hand. "La Reina has been with me for thirty years. She is my special good luck charm for the blackjack table."

"But Abuelita, won't you need her yourself?"

She pointed to her leg. "I won't be going to the casino anytime soon, even to pick up my thirty-five dollars in chips. Did I tell you? They are finally going to mail me a check, that casino. For my thirty-five dollars. You put La Reina in your pocket, and soon when I fly to Washington, you will show me where you defeated that gato estúpido. Yes?"

El gato estupido. The stupid cat. I looked at the playing card with the red lady wearing the triangle crown, holding the blue flower. She seemed to be telling me, "You can do it, Fina. We can do it." Maybe we could. I did feel stronger, braver, smarter than the Demon Cat. I would solve the mystery and break the curse of the stupid cat. "I will do it, Abuelita. I promise. I'll be brave and I will face the Demon Cat."

I put the torn card in my pocket. "I'll take good care of her, Abuelita."

Chapter Twenty Seven

Thanksgiving weekend was over before I knew it. I had Trina's pink cowboy boots from the clothing swap, and she had my Washington Nationals jersey. We were still best friends. That made me less homesick. I had this dumb idea that everyone in L.A. had forgotten who I was, that Trina had made a new best friend, and it wasn't me. Now that I had seen Trina and my old school and even our old house, I was ready to go back to Washington.

We sat around the airport terminal, waiting for our group to be called. Papa stared at his phone, tapping away at an email. Gabby sat two seats away, texting her friends on the family phone–probably telling them about how mean Papa was since she was grounded for a month and had to finish unpacking all the boxes by herself as her punishment for crunching Tío Tom's bumper.

I reached into my pocket and felt the smooth edges of the queen of hearts. "Get ready, gato estúpido," I said to myself. "I'm ready for you."

•　　　　　•　　　　　•

It was teeth-chattering chilly when we got back to Washington, the first really cold weather since we moved. Papa said I was cold because I didn't wear my scarf. Everybody wore scarves in Washington. Everybody. The mail lady, the garbage man, even the President. When I saw people on TV wearing scarves, I thought they looked stupid. Nobody wore scarves in California. Neither did I. Gabby was wearing hers. She gave me a look and stuck out her tongue. I stuck mine out at her.

We were waiting for the subway at the airport. Gabby said we should take a cab, but Papa said unless she was paying for it–and since her entire allowance for the next ten years would be going to pay for the repair of Tío Tom's car–we would take the Metro. Most of the subway was underground, but at Reagan National Airport, the tracks were high above the road. Standing up there on the platform with the wind blowing made the night even more frigid. I knew that vocabulary word without Becka's help or Michael's dictionary.

"Papa, is it frigid enough to snow?" I asked.

Papa looked up from his phone and laughed. "Not yet, mija."

I shivered. But I knew it wasn't just from the cold. I was also thinking about the Demon Cat.

•   •   •

The next morning was raining and cold and the day was dark and gray.

"Fina, do you know the answer?"

I snapped to attention. What was Ms. Greenwood talking about? Oh yeah, the difference between lakes and oceans. I was about to say "salt" but she called on Becka instead.

Even though it was raining, I took a detour to Papa's office by walking past the smokers' park on top of the parking garage. I thought maybe I could "accidentally" run into Senator Something. I wondered who was walking him these days. All I knew was that it wasn't me. I just wanted to see him again, to let him know that I hadn't abandoned him. That I still cared about him.

I wanted to tell Senator Something that I knew what I had to do: confront the Demon Cat. I would explain to my furry friend that I had to go down to the Crypt and offer myself as bait, waiting for whatever it was to come out of hiding and find me. I would tell him about Abuelita's La Reina card, but I wouldn't show it to him because I didn't want him to slobber all over it.

There was no one in the park. I sighed. I felt in my pocket for the queen of hearts. She was there, safe and dry. But without Senator Something's blessing, I wasn't sure of my plan. Maybe I could go to the Crypt tomorrow. Maybe next week. I was too wet and too cold ... and okay, I admitted, too scared to do it tonight.

•   •   •

Gabby was unpacking boxes when Papa and I got home from Capitol Hill. "Change your clothes," she scolded, sounding like Abuelita. "Both of you. You'll catch pneumonia!"

Papa laughed and took our dripping wet raincoats and umbrellas out to the back porch. Gabby didn't say it in a mean voice. Even though she was grounded, Gabby seemed happier since our trip to Los Angeles. I paused on the stairs. Gabby was actually humming.

"Was it worth it?" I asked her. "Driving?"

Gabby's face broke into the biggest smile imaginable. "Oh, yes," she said. "Every minute of it."

•   •   •

Abuelita called after dinner. She talked to Papa and then she talked to Gabby. When it was my turn, she said, "Guess who's coming to Washington for Christmas?"

"For Christmas? Really, Abuelita?"

"That knucklehead doctor of mine finally took off my cast. I have been telling him for weeks that I can feel the bones healing. He never believed me. Until he took another X-ray and saw for himself. I can almost run a marathon! Well, not quite. Not yet, anyway. I still have to go to physical therapy. But I can do that in Washington as easily as I can in Los Angeles."

"So you're really coming, Abuelita. Finally."

"Finally." Then she whispered into the phone, "So.

What have you done about your Demon Cat?"

I told her I hadn't done anything yet. I was thinking of a strategy. Maybe more research.

"The time for preparation is over, mija. It is time for action."

And so it was. Tomorrow I would finally confront that gato estupido.

Chapter Twenty Eight

I wore two pairs of tights and my gloves and my coat and my furry hat. But I was still cold when Papa walked me to school the next morning. "You could wear your scarf, you know," Papa said. I kissed him goodbye and ran up the steps to St. Philip's.

At recess, Michael showed me his secret weapon against the cold: backpacker hand warmers. You tear open a little package and the minute the cold air reaches the little tea bag inside, it starts to heat up. Michael said the iron inside the bag starts to rust and that creates the heat. Warm hands and a science lesson in one package. And no stupid looking scarf.

I wished I had one of Michael's hand warmers for my walk to the Capitol after school. The rain had stopped. The storm had knocked a lot of the leaves off the trees in the park. The oaks looked spooky with just the bare branches against the dark gray sky.

I stopped by the Rules Committee room, where Papa was meeting with a bunch of tall congressmen in blue suits. They kept waving their arms and talking loudly. As usual, Papa stood with his head tilted to the side, listening. Claudia was busy writing down everything in her notebook, scribbling a hundred miles an hour. I waved at them and dumped my backpack with a staffer. It was just as well that Papa was busy. I didn't want him to worry.

As I waited for the elevator that would take me to the first floor, I felt around in my pocket for La Reina. Where was she? Maybe the other pocket. I looked inside. There she was! The elevator dinged. I automatically stepped forward without looking, and bumped into a lady stepping out. "Sorry, ma'am," I said.

I looked up. It was Congresswoman Mitchell.

She frowned and said, "I'm late for a meeting. But please stop by to see me tomorrow after school, Ms. Mendoza. We have something to discuss. Oh, and here." She reached into her purse and handed me the squeaky toy shaped like the Washington Monument. "I believe this belongs to you."

My heart sank to my stomach. Senator Something's toy. If she was giving it back, then it was official: my dog walking days were over. Senator Something was off limits.

I nodded my head at the congresswoman and shoved the dog toy into my coat pocket. I stepped into the elevator and pushed the button. Well, I could wait until later to be sad about Senator Something. Right now, I had a mission to accomplish. It was time to confront the Demon Cat.

I didn't enter the Crypt right away. I walked around the corner to the bust of Winston Churchill. I touched his nose.

"We still are masters of our fate," I said, just like

Papa. "We still are captain of our souls." Between Mr. Churchill and the queen of hearts, I was prepared.

I walked boldly into the Crypt. It was empty and quiet and dim. I sat on the bench and waited. I thought about curses, about Abuelita's broken leg, about Gabby's car crash, about Senator Something getting hit by the car. I thought about moth invasions and exploding spaghetti sauce and squashed banana on Mama's picture and stepping on sidewalk cracks.

And then something surprised me: I wasn't scared anymore. I thought about all of our bad luck. Had it really been a curse? Gabby had crashed the car because she was impatient to drive. I dropped the spaghetti sauce jar because I was in a hurry. Senator Something got hit by the car because I didn't hold tight to the leash. Abuelita broke her leg because–well, I wasn't sure exactly why she fell off the barstool, but I knew it wasn't because of el gato estupido.

I stuck my hand in my pocket. Abuelita's La Reina, the queen of hearts, was there. It was as if Abuelita was there with me. I stood a little taller. I was Fina Mendoza, granddaughter of Josefina Mendoza, daughter of Congressman Arturo Mendoza and Grace Mendoza. I was double digits, ten years old, not a baby. Even Congresswoman Mitchell, who would be mad at me until the end of time, called me Ms. Mendoza. I could do this. I would figure out the mystery of the Demon Cat.

And then I heard it: the banging sound behind the air conditioning grate. I froze, standing as still as the statue of Robert E. Lee. I held my breath. The banging stopped. I climbed up on the wooden bench next to the wall, but I was still too short to see anything inside the grate.

And then I heard it. It wasn't a hiss this time. It was a mouth noise, the kind Trina's cat Pixie makes when she watches birds out the window. It was the same sound I heard the first time I encountered the Demon Cat.

"Mrreowow!"

Where was it coming from?

I jumped down from the bench. I listened hard. There was a faint click, click of tiny toenails on the stone floor. I scanned the gloom of the room, looking for shadows among the stone statues. Was it? Yes! There behind the statue of Crawford W. Long, the man who discovered ether, the stuff that knocked people out for an operation, I saw a long, black tail. It slowly waved back and forth, making giant question marks in the air. I held my breath and waited. A furry black creature peeked out from behind the marble base. The animal crept along the floor, its belly flat to the ground, scooting along on the stones. The Demon Cat! It was real!

It wasn't gigantic, but its shadow was. The flick of its tail played tricks on my eyes, the question mark shadow bouncing around the arches of the Crypt.

I didn't move. I wasn't sure what to do next. Should I reason with it? Beg it to leave the Mendoza family alone? Tell it to go curse somebody else? I could shout, "Begone, Demon!" or try to capture it with my coat or just hold up La Reina and see if she was powerful enough to send the cat back to whatever corner of hell it had come from.

But the Demon Cat wasn't paying attention to me. It focused every bit of its attention on someone or something else along the curved wall. I followed the cat's stare. I could see nothing. But the Demon Cat could. "Mrreowow," it whined.

I felt like my hair was standing up straight, pushing my headband up over my ears.

Suddenly, the Demon Cat leaped. Its head, then its body, and finally its tail, disappeared into a dark, shadowy corner of the Crypt. I heard a scuffle and a tiny cry and more scuffling noises. I wanted to run away before the Demon Cat attacked me, but I was frozen.

Then, it was silent. Eventually, I heard soft marshmallow footsteps. The creature emerged from the shadows. There she was: the Demon Cat, in the flesh. Or at least, in the fur. Was she real? Was I jinxed for life? I didn't move, not even to reach into my pocket to touch the queen of hearts.

She looked at me. I looked at her. Closely. The Demon Cat wasn't the size of a bus. Her eyes didn't glow bright yellow. She was just a big cat. And she had a mouse in her mouth.

The cat marched over to me and dropped the mouse at my feet. A present. She looked up at me, very proud of herself. She "mrreowowed" again. It wasn't a threatening mrreowow. It seemed more like an "aren't I clever" mrreowow.

Was it possible that I could understand cats as well

as I understood Senator Something? I thought about the gift-mouse. If the Demon Cat was giving me a present, she wasn't mad at me. And if she wasn't mad at me, she wouldn't be cursing me, sending bad luck my way. Would she?

The cat sat there politely on the polished stone floor, looking up at me. Waiting. What did she want? "Thank you," I told her.

She nodded, as if to say, "You may approach." I leaned down to pet her head. I figured maybe a cat would like that as much as Senator Something. But as I stretched out my hand, the cat growled. It was that same angry "mrreowow."

I pulled my hand back. What had I done? Maybe I had moved too quickly. The cat didn't move. I tried again, reaching my hand over her head to reach her ears. She sniffed my hand. Once again, she growled and hissed at me.

What was wrong with my hand? What had I been touching? I stuck my hands in my pockets and found Senator Something's chew toy.

And then I figured it out: my hand had the smell of dog on it. Of course! It wasn't me, it was the smell of dog that made her mad. She wasn't mad at me. She was mad at Senator Something. She wasn't a mythical Demon Cat, she was a real cat who hated real dogs.

"I see you met D.C."

I hadn't heard the footsteps. There in the archway was that janitor who worked for the Architect of the Capitol, the one wearing the blue polo shirt with AOC on the pocket, the one who had been cleaning fingerprints off the plastic cases in the Crypt and putting yellow tape in the corners of the Rules Committee room.

"D.C.?" I asked. Just like the initials on my detective notebook. "Her name is Demon Cat?"

"District of Columbia," he said. He rubbed the cat's head and pulled on her ears. She purred. I was right about one thing. Both she and Senator Something liked having their ears pulled.

"Good girl," he said to the cat. Then he stuck out his big hand. "Name's Carl Jefferson."

"Fina Mendoza," I said, shaking his hand. "Nice to meet you. Is she your cat?"

"I suppose. Much as a cat can belong to anybody." But it was easy to see that the cat really liked this particular man, rubbing up against his blue work trousers.

"And she lives here?" I asked. "In the Crypt?"

He nodded. He used a paper towel to pick up the dead mouse and dropped it in the trash can. "Guess you could say she works here, too."

He squirted something blue from a bottle and wiped the floor where the mouse had been walking.

"Always been mice in the Capitol. Generations of mice. They still think they have the run of the place. But lawmakers don't like that, so we gotta get rid of them. The mice, that is, not the congressmen. Upstairs, we use those yellow sticky traps."

"Like the ones you stuck in all the corners of the Rules Committee room?"

Mr. Jefferson nodded. So that's what explained the weird yellow tape.

"The bosses don't want us to use old-fashioned mousetraps," he said.

"Like the ones in cartoons?" I pictured those metal contraptions with a giant piece of cheese.

"Right," he said. "Too cruel. What those do-gooders don't know is that the mouse is usually alive when he gets stuck to the tape. Still alive when you go back to collect them in the morning, stuck to the paper, crying and scared. Terrified little critter. Then it's up to me to get rid of it."

"You mean, you have to kill it," I said.

He nodded sadly. I felt sorry for those mice. "Can't you just set them free?"

"They'd come right back here to the nice, warm Capitol."

"How come you don't use the sticky tape here in the Crypt?" I asked.

"Too many school kids with too many busy fingers in the Crypt," he said. "You know one of them even broke the National Mall table."

I looked at the floor. "That was me," I said.

"You?"

"Well actually, it was Senator Something."

"Is he that new freshman senator from Kansas?" he asked.

"No. He's a dog," I said. "I used to walk him for Congresswoman Mitchell. He bit off one of the Washington Monuments."

"Hmph," said Mr. Jefferson. "That there National Mall table was D.C.'s favorite place to perch. She'd sit right in the middle, lookin' around the room for mice."

I thought about D.C. hissing when she smelled Senator Something on my hand. I'll bet Senator Something smelled cat on the National Mall table! That's why he jumped up there and took a bite out of–

I decided to change the subject. "Where did D.C. come from?"

The janitor reached down and scratched the cat's ears again. The cat purred. "Found this here feline nosing around the garbage room in the basement. Didn't belong to nobody. So I brought her to work. Daytime, she sleeps up there." He pointed to the air conditioning duct. "Nighttime, she comes out and goes to work here in the Crypt. D.C. is a first-class mouser. Just don't tell nobody. 'Specially that Capitol policewoman."

I looked at Mr. Jefferson. He smiled. "You know the one. Mean as spit. That woman hates anything that ain't in the rule book. 'Specially animals. Dogs, cats, kids, hates 'em all."

He looked around the Crypt, leaned over and whispered, "So I told her a little story."

"Let me guess, Mr. Jefferson. You told the policewoman that the Demon Cat of Capitol Hill had returned to the Crypt! You told her D.C. was the Demon Cat!"

He chuckled. "Everybody around here knows the legend of the Demon Cat of Capitol Hill. Nobody believes it. Except her."

And me, I thought. Or at least I did. Until now.

"That policewoman, she's bad news," he said. "Lookin' for trouble. But long as she thinks the Demon Cat is out to get her, she'll leave me and D.C. alone."

"Mrreowow," agreed the cat.

I was still trying to put all the pieces together. The Demon Cat was real. She wasn't putting a curse on me, she just smelled dog. All of our months of bad luck were just—what? Old fashioned bad luck? Careless mistakes like picking up the spaghetti sauce jar with wet hands or Abuelita forgetting she was sitting on a barstool at the casino? Or me not holding onto Senator Something's leash the way the dog walking lady showed me. There was no curse. Not really. There was no such thing as a Demon Cat of Capitol Hill.

D.C. rubbed up against my leg. It was like she was saying, "You finally figured it out, Fina. Good girl. Good girl."

Cats can be so annoying. They think they know everything. Kind of like Becka.

I could hardly wait to tell Papa and Abuelita and Trina: I had solved the mystery of the Demon Cat.

Chapter Twenty Nine

The sun was so bright the next morning, I needed my sunglasses. But unlike back in California, I also needed a tee shirt under my school uniform and two pairs of gloves. Brr.

It was hard to concentrate on prefixes and suffixes when the only suffix I could think about was the one at the end of "punishment." All during math, I kept wondering whether I could find some other dog to walk to earn the $360 it would take to repair the broken Washington Monument. All during history, I kept thinking of my meeting later that afternoon with Congresswoman Mitchell–maybe the last time in my life that I would ever see Senator Something. In religion class, I didn't even notice that Ms. Greenwood had called on me until Becka poked me in the back, whispering, "Wake up, snooze head!"

After school, I walked slowly from St. Phillip's to Capitol Hill, turning my face to catch as much sunshine as possible. But the sunny day outside didn't reach my insides. I was cold with dread. I stuck Senator Something's squeaky toy in my pocket, along with La Reina, just for luck.

The familiar barrel of peanuts was by the front door

of Congresswoman Mitchell's office. I didn't want one. I wasn't hungry. John, the staffer who drove the car that hit Senator Something wasn't sitting in his usual place at the front desk. Maybe he was fired. I guess Congresswoman Mitchell was going to fire me, too.

"She'll be with you in a minute," said the girl at John's desk. "Take a seat."

I sat on the couch. My stomach churned. On the wall, I saw a picture of Senator Something licking the face of Congresswoman Mitchell. It must have been an election night, with all the red, white, and blue balloons floating over the stage. She looked very happy. So did Senator Something.

The door to Congresswoman Mitchell's office opened. "You can go in now," said the girl at the desk.

I took a deep breath. I reached in my pocket and touched the squeaky toy and La Reina. "You can do this," I told myself. "You faced down the Demon Cat of Capitol Hill all by yourself, you can face up to your punishment."

The congresswoman's inner office was painted deep blue, the color of Gabby's blue bananas. That made me smile a little bit. My smile disappeared when I spotted Senator Something lying on an oversized doggie bed next to the congresswoman's desk. His back leg was wrapped up in a purple brace with Velcro straps. I know he saw me because his raggedy tail started thumping on the carpet. He wanted to get up and come over to me, but I shook my head. Senator Something seemed sad, and put his head down on his paws.

"Take a seat, Ms. Mendoza." Congresswoman

Mitchell pointed to the couch. John, the receptionist, was already sitting there. He nodded at me. No one was smiling. I sat.

"John told me what happened, how he should have been looking when he pulled out of the Rayburn garage, how he might have been speeding," she said.

John hung his head. He felt as bad as me.

"But of course," she continued, "John wouldn't have hit Senator Something if you had been properly doing your job, Ms. Mendoza."

I looked down at the carpet. I think I heard Senator Something whimper in sympathy.

Congresswoman Mitchell sighed. "I was furious with both of you," she said. "I needed some time to cool off. I love that silly old hound dog." Senator Something wagged his tail. He knew she was talking about him. She walked over and scratched his ears. Then she faced both of us.

"It's clear that Senator Something loves you, Ms. Mendoza. He doesn't blame you for his accident. Or John. I believe everybody deserves a second chance. What say you and I start all over again?"

"You mean, you don't want to fire John and me?" I asked.

"No, I don't." She looked at John. "Who would answer my phones?" She looked at me. "And who would walk my dog?"

I didn't know what to say. Was she offering me my old job back? I looked at Senator Something, who seemed to be saying, "Yup."

"What about the bill from the animal hospital?"

"Well, Senator Something is my dog, so the vet bill is my problem. Do we have a deal, Ms. Mendoza?" She put out her hand. I shook it. "Now, we have another matter to settle. John, do you have a copy of that invoice?"

John handed a piece of paper to the congresswoman.

"Invoice for repair of Washington Monument on National Mall display table," she read. "$360."

"Don't worry, Ma'am," I said. "I promised to pay for it. And I will. Eventually."

"Yes, well I appreciate you taking responsibility for the expense, but it's not entirely your fault. I believe it was my dog who caused the damage. Suppose we split it. Fifty-fifty?"

"Really?" I asked.

"Let's see." The congresswoman started scribbling numbers down on a pad of paper on her desk. "Your portion would be $180. Which, I believe is the amount you have earned so far walking Senator Something. Yes?"

I nodded.

"Then I think we can call it even and start again with a clean slate." Politicians always use phrases like that–"clean slate." That means a fresh start.

"Thank you, Congresswoman Mitchell!"

Senator Something barked.

"Go on, Senator Something," said the lawmaker, "go seal the deal."

Senator Something crossed the room on three legs almost as fast as if he had four working ones. I met him halfway with open arms. There was a lot of dog slobbering as he told me how glad he was that we were friends again. I reached in my pocket for the squeak toy and held it in front of his nose. "One condition, Senator Something," I told him. "This is the only Washington Monument you are allowed to chew." He barked in agreement.

Chapter Thirty

Gabby made some goopy oatmeal for breakfast. Papa poured himself a cup of coffee and announced, "I've got a surprise, mijas. Warm coats, cute hats, be ready at my office at four."

Papa was rarely mysterious. Gabby rolled her eyes. Papa's "surprise" was probably another night of smiling at strangers and getting your hand squeezed too hard by some politician, or standing around on sore feet, posing for pictures with Papa.

After walking Senator Something, I met Gabby at Papa's office at four o'clock on the dot. Something clearly was up. Everybody was smiling. Papa's receptionist was even humming, "God Rest Ye Merry Gentleman." Papa breezed out of his office in the back. "Let's go," he said.

We followed Papa to the elevator, down to the ground floor, past the X-ray machines at the Independence Avenue door and kept walking.

"Where are we going?" Gabby complained. "I have geometry homework."

"You'll see."

We crossed the street and hiked over the dying grass to the foot of Capitol Hill, near the statue of Ulysses S.

Grant, the Civil War general who sat on his horse and seemed to be protecting the Capitol from any Confederate soldiers who might still be wandering around Washington. It was yet another cold afternoon, but I refused to wear a scarf again, even though Gabby had offered me one of hers. My ears were cold, but I still think scarves look dumb.

Suddenly, Papa stopped. "Look!"

We looked. Papa gestured to the Capitol, all lit up, glowing and white. The only light that wasn't turned on was the one on top that told the world that Congress was voting. On the lawn in front of the Capitol was a gigantic tree. A Christmas tree.

"*Our* Christmas tree, mijas."

What did Papa mean "our" tree?

"Ladies and gentlemen!" A man in a suit stood on a small stage near the tree and talked into a microphone. He wasn't even wearing a coat. Wasn't he cold? Papa shooed us over toward the stage.

"I have the honor of introducing the Speaker of the House."

A man in a big overcoat and an orangey face and a blue scarf stepped up to the microphone. People clapped.

"Who cares?" Gabby said.

The Speaker gestured down toward Papa. "First of all, I'd like to introduce the man whose district once was home to this lovely white fir tree. Congressman Arturo Mendoza represents the great 34th congressional district of Los Angeles. Now, many of you might think of L.A.

as nothing but freeways and cars and traffic. Congressman Mendoza's district stretches all the way up to the Angeles National Forest, in the mountains above L.A."

Papa climbed the stairs to the platform. He smiled and gave a little wave as people in the audience below applauded.

"Great. It's a tree," said Gabby. "Big deal. It's cold. When do we get to go home?"

Apparently not right away. The Speaker had more to say. "It's an appropriate theme for this year's Capitol Christmas Tree, given the fact that Democrats and Republicans have been fighting this year like–well, like cats and dogs."

The Speaker laughed at what he thought was a pretty funny joke. A few people laughed, too. Papa just smiled. The Speaker and Papa were from different parties. They don't laugh at each other's jokes. I looked at Gabby. What was going on? She shrugged her shoulders.

The Speaker then gestured to Gabby and me. "The congressman is accompanied by his two lovely daughters–" He looked at a piece of paper in his hand. "Gabrielle and Josefina Mendoza," he announced into the microphone.

Us!

People started clapping. Papa waved at us to join him on the stage. The Speaker shook Papa's hand and patted him on the back. He smiled and nodded to Gabby. And then–he wasn't going to–he did! He actually patted me on the head. I hated that.

His hand smelled familiar. Like a cigarette. No, a cigar! The same cigar smoke I'd smelled in the Crypt. Of course! The Speaker's office was right upstairs from the Crypt. It was him who was smoking. Another mystery solved.

Papa stepped to the microphone. "The people of Southern California are honored to share one of our beautiful white firs with the nation as this year's Capitol Christmas Tree," he said. "Though as a California native, this poor old guy can't quite understand why it's so darned cold out here in Washington."

People laughed and clapped. I looked out at the audience. It was mostly staffers and reporters and a few tourists. One of the kids in the crowd waved at me. It was Michael! He was bundled up in a puffy jacket and a red knit hat and scarf. He stood near one of the reporters staring into a camera, waiting to talk live to some anchor person back in the studio. Michael pointed and mouthed "my father" and made a face. I laughed. That would make Becka jealous. Her mom worked for a senator, but Michael's dad was the one who talked to senators and congressmen on TV.

The Speaker returned to the microphone. "And now…" I could tell that he was warming up for another speech. It was getting even colder. I stomped my feet.

"Would the congressman's two lovely daughters–" You could tell he already forgot our names. A staffer whispered in his ear to remind him. "Gabrielle and Josefina, step over here and do the honors?" He gestured to a large button next to the podium. Gabby and I looked at each other.

The crowd below began counting. "Three, two, one!" We slammed our hands down on the button at the same time. Cameras flashed. "Oh, Christmas Tree" started playing over the loudspeaker. And behind us, the gigantic tree lit up, every inch of it covered with blue and red and orange and green and yellow lights. It was beautiful!

Then little bits of paper started floating down from the sky, like the ash after a brush fire in the hills above Los Angeles. Could it be that the Capitol was on fire? I sniffed. It didn't smell like a brush fire. Was it confetti? One of the white bits landed on my nose. It was cold. It was wet. It was–

"Snow, Gabby! Papa, it's snowing!"

Fat flakes swirled all around us. Gabby tried to catch a handful to throw at me, but it was too soon for snowballs. I stuck out my tongue. The snowflakes tasted like little bits of ice. I could hardly wait to tell Trina: it was finally snowing in Washington. Maybe it would last until Christmas when Abuelita arrived. We could show her the snow and show her our own Capitol Christmas tree!

"Did you notice the ornaments, mija?" Papa whispered in my ear.

We scrambled down the stairs, Papa shaking hands with a million people. "Got a minute, Congressman for an interview?" asked Michael's father. I sighed. But Papa told Michael's father. "I'd love to, Jack, but a little later. I have something very important to do at the moment."

Papa put an arm around Gabby and one around me. "Race you!" he said. The three of us sprinted to the tree. Gabby got there first. "Check it out, Fina," she said. "Cars!"

Handmade ornaments hung on all the branches. There were lots and lots of racing cars. Gabby kept pointing at this one and that one, calling out "Porche" and "Jaguar" and "classic Stingray" as she identified each ornament. Some were harder to figure out than others. Some barely looked like cars.

"Kids in schools all over the district made every one of them," said Papa.

The snow started to stick to the branches. Patches of white covered the dead grass. Bits of snow sparkled, as if glitter had been sprinkled all over everything. Our Capitol Christmas tree was beginning to look like the trees on Christmas cards.

I looked closer at the other ornaments. There weren't just cars hanging on the limbs. I looked at Papa. He nodded and smiled. Some of the ornaments were dogs, and some were cats.

Papa pointed to a sparkly ornament with curly orange fur on it shaped into a funny looking orange pooch. "There's Senator Something," he said. It wasn't a very good dog, but the goofy look on his face looked a lot like Senator Something. There were other dog ornaments, too–a German Shepherd that looked like Hans the police dog, a golden dog that looked like

Buster, the guide dog, and a shaggy little white mutt that looked like Bruin. There were lots of cats, too–gray striped tabbies and a tuxedo cat like Trina's cat Pixie. Dogs and cats and cars.

"How did you know, Papa?" I asked.

"I do pay attention to my girls once in a while," he said, brushing bits of snow from my hair. "Look," he said, pointing. "There's your Demon Cat."

And there, inside a round glass ball, staring straight at me, was a skinny black cat with yellow eyes. The ornament was pretty big, but the cat still wasn't the size of a school bus.

I squeezed Papa's hand.

"Don't be silly, Papa," I told him. "There's no such thing as a Demon Cat."

About the Author

Kitty Felde hosts the award-winning *Book Club for Kids* podcast – named one of the top 10 kidcasts in the world by "The Times of London." She also writes plays that are performed worldwide. She fell in love with literature for young readers when she was a young reader herself, working at her local public library. Kitty looked for the Demon Cat while covering Congress for public radio. She found the paw prints, but not the cat.

Many, many people took Fina into their hearts and encouraged us on the path to publication. Thank you. We couldn't have done it without you.

In particular, thanks to the many members of California's congressional delegation for sharing their stories, especially Congresswoman Linda Sanchez and her son Joaquin, the earliest readers of this book. Thanks as well to Congressman David Valadao whose office had the best treat in the House: chocolate milk from the many dairy farms in his district. Thanks to Congressman David Dreier, former chair of the House Rules Committee who loves those *plein air* paintings. And thanks to Congresswoman Grace Napolitano, Abuelita to most of Capitol Hill and smuggler of Mexican food to most of the House.

Thanks to Steve Livengood from the U.S. Capitol Historical Society for separating fact from fiction and to Mary Freed for her tales of Halloween on Capitol Hill. And thanks to the many staffers on Capitol Hill who work for the Rules Committee, the House Historian's office, the Architect of the Capitol, the Office of Congressional Accessibility Services, as well as staffers for Congressman Alan Lowenthal, who let me camp out in Fina's "girl cave" across the hallway, and to all the kind and friendly folks in the House and Senate press galleries.

Thanks to my wonderful writing community: Ellen Struve, a marvelous playwright and ever-supportive Skype writing compadre. I'm blessed with two SCBWI critique groups: Friederike Ahrens, Larry Fogel-Bublick, Lauren Greenberg, Mary Rose Janya, Amy Javaid, Don Jewler, Ginger Park, Elaine Pirozzi, Daniela Rodrigues, and Jess Stork. Thank you all. And thanks to Angele McQuade, who carved out a writing community at whatever Ballston coffee joint would put up with us. Thanks to my agent Eric Myers who championed the book against great odds. And to my cat Chessie who always has a lot to say about everything.

And of course, thanks to the young woman who inspires me every day and lent her name to the book, Fina Martinez.

Most of all, thanks to my number one cheerleader, editor, fellow writer, and beloved husband Tad Daley. I'm the luckiest girl to have you in my life.